Publisher's note

Ancient Chinese classic poems are exquisite works of art. As far as 2,000 years ago, Chinese poets composed the beautiful work *Book of Poetry* and *Elegies of the South*. Later, they created more splendid Tang poetry and Song lyrics. Such classic works as *Thus Spoke the Master* and *Laws Divine and Human* were extremely significant in building and shaping the culture of the Chinese nation. These works are both a cultural bond linking the thoughts and affections of Chinese people and an important bridge for Chinese culture and the world.

Mr. Xu Yuanchong has been engaged in translation for 70 years. He won the Lifetime Achievement Award in Translation conferred by the Translators Association of China (TAC) in 2010, and won the "Aurora Borealis" Prize for Outstanding Translation of Fiction Literature, conferred by the Federation of International Translators (FIT) in 2014. He is honored as the only expert who translates Chinese poems into both English and French. After his excellent interpretation, many Chinese classic poems have been further refined into perfect English and French rhymes. This collection of Classical Chinese Poetry and Prose gathers his most representative English translations. It includes the classic works *Thus Spoke the Master*, *Laws Divine and Human* and dramas such as *Romance of the Western Bower*, *Dream in Peony Pavilion*, *Love in Long-life Hall* and *Peach Blooms Painted with Blood*. The largest part of the collection includes the translation of selected poems from different dynasties. The selection includes various types of poetry. The selected works start from the pre-Qin era to the Qing Dynasty, covering almost the entire history of classic poems in China. Reading these works is like tasting "living water from the source" of Chinese culture.

We hope this collection will help English readers "understand, enjoy and delight in" Chinese classic poems, share the intelligence of Confucius and Lao Tzu (the Older Master), share the gracefulness of Tang poems, Song lyrics and classic operas and songs and promote exchanges between Eastern and Western culture. We also sincerely invite precious suggestions from our readers.

出版前言

中国古代经典诗文是中国传统文化的奇葩。早在两千多年以前,中国诗人就写出了美丽的《诗经》和《楚辞》;以后,他们又创造了更加灿烂的唐诗和宋词。《论语》《老子》这样的经典著作,则在塑造、构成中华民族文化精神方面具有极其重要的意义。这些作品既是联接所有中国人思想、情感的文化纽带,也是中国文化走向世界的重要桥梁。

许渊冲先生从事翻译工作70年,2010年荣获"中国翻译文化终身成就奖",2014年荣获国际译联颁发的"北极光"杰出文学翻译奖。他被称为将中国诗词译成英法韵文的唯一专家,经他的妙手,许多中国经典诗文被译成出色的英文和法文韵语。这套"许译中国经典诗文集"荟萃许先生最具代表性的英文译作,既包括《论语》《老子》这样的经典著作,又包括《西厢记》《牡丹亭》《长生殿》《桃花扇》等戏曲剧本,数量最多的则是历代诗歌选集。这些诗歌选集包括诗、词、散曲等多种体裁,所选作品上起先秦,下至清代,几乎涵盖了中国古典诗歌的整个历史。阅读和了解这些作品,即可尽览中国文化的"源头活水"。

我们希望这套许氏译本能使英语读者对中国经典诗文也"知之,好之,乐之",能够分享孔子、老子的智慧,分享唐诗、宋词、中国古典戏曲的优美,并以此促进东西文化的交流。也敬请读者朋友提出宝贵意见。

PROJECT FOR TRANSLATION AND PUBLICATION
OF CHINESE CULTURAL WORKS
中国文化著作翻译出版工程项目

CLASSICAL CHINESE POETRY AND PROSE

300 YUAN SONGS

TRANSLATED BY XU YUANCHONG

许译中国经典诗文集

元曲三百首 | 许渊冲 译

五洲传播出版社　　中华书局
China Intercontinental Press　　Zhonghua Book Company

Contents
目　　录

Preface 1   序　　 195
Yuan Haowen   元好问
   Man And Moon   人月圆：卜居外家东园
     (I) 8   （一）......................201
     (II) 8   （二）...................... 201
   Minor Sacred Music   小圣乐：骤雨打新荷
     (I) 9   （一）......................201
     (II) 9   （二）......................202
Yang Guo   杨果
   Red Peach Blossoms   小桃红：采莲女
     (I) 10   （一）......................202
     (II) 10   （二）......................202
Liu Bingzhong   刘秉忠
   Dried Lotus Leaves   干荷叶
     (I) 11   （一）......................203

(II) 11

(III) 12

Du Renjie

Playing the Child (I) 13

(II) 13

(III) 14

(IV) 14

(V) 15

(VI) 15

(VII) 16

(VIII) 16

Wang Heqing

A Drinker's Sky 17

Half and Half (I) 17

(II) 18

(III) 18

He Xicun

Red Peach Blossoms (I) 19

(II) 19

(III) 20

Shang Ting

Song of Princess Pan 20

（二）....................................... 203

（三）....................................... 203

杜仁杰

耍孩儿（一）...................... 204

（二）....................................... 204

（三）....................................... 204

（四）....................................... 205

（五）....................................... 205

（六）....................................... 205

（七）....................................... 206

（八）....................................... 206

王和卿

醉中天................................... 206

一半儿：题情（一）...... 207

（二）....................................... 207

（三）....................................... 207

盍西村

小桃红：江岸水灯........... 207

小桃红：客船晚烟........... 208

小桃红：杂咏..................... 208

商挺

潘妃曲................................... 208

Hu Zhiyu
Intoxicated in East Wind..... 21
Bo Yan
Welcome to Spring............21
Wang Yun
Joy of Calm Lake...............22
Lu Zhi
Higher and Higher............22

Intoxicated in East Wind (I)... 23

(II) 23

(III) 24

Song of Moon Palace

(I)....................................24

(II) 25

Joy before Palace.................26
Chen Cao'an
Sheep on the Slope............27
Guan Hanqing
Song of White Crane..........28

Four Pieces of Jade:

Parting Grief 28

Four Pieces of Jade (I) 29

(II) 29

胡祗遹
沉醉东风..............................209
伯颜
喜春来................................ 209
王恽
平湖乐..................................209
卢挚
节节高..................................210

沉醉东风：秋景................210

沉醉东风：闲居................210

沉醉东风：春情................211

蟾宫曲：扬州汪右丞席上即事

....211

蟾宫曲：醉赠乐府珠帘秀...211

殿前欢...................................212
陈草庵
山坡羊..................................212
关汉卿
白鹤子..................................212

四块玉：别情

....213

四块玉：闲适（一）....213

（二）....... 213

Intoxicated in East Wind...30

Song of Great Virtue (I) ...30

(II) 31

Green Jade Flute (I) 31

(II) 32

A Sprig of Flowers (I) 33

(II) 33

(III) 35

(IV) 36

Bai Pu

Parasite Grass 38

Song of Spring...................38

Sunny Sand (I) 39

(II) 39

(III) 40

(IV) 40

Intoxicated in East Wind...41

Yao Sui

Drinking Song 41

Leaning on Balustrade 42

Yu Tianxi

From Falling Swan (I) 42

沉醉东风.......................213

大德歌（一）...............214

（二）..........................214

碧玉箫（一）...............214

（二）..........................214

一枝花（一）...............215

（二）..........................215

（三）..........................216

（四）..........................216

白朴

寄生草..........................217

阳春曲..........................217

天净沙（一）...............217

（二）..........................217

（三）..........................218

（四）..........................218

沉醉东风.......................218

姚燧

醉高歌..........................218

凭阑人..........................219

庾天锡

雁儿落过得胜令（一）...219

(II) 43

Liu Minzhong

Varnished Black Bow 43

Ma Zhiyuan

Four Pieces of Jade (I) 44

(II) 44

Sunny Sand 45

Song of Clear River (I) 45

(II) 46

Song of Long-lived Sun (I) .. 46

(II) 47

(III) 47

Song of Long-lived Sun 48

Autumn Thoughts (I) 48

(II) 49

(III) 49

(IV) 50

(V) 50

(VI) 51

(VII) 51

Zhao Mengfu

Backyard Flowers 52

（二）................................219

刘敏中

黑漆弩....................................220

马致远

四块玉：浔阳江.................220

四块玉：叹世......................220

天净沙...................................221

清江引：野兴（一）.......221

（二）....................................221

寿阳曲（一）.....................221

（二）....................................222

（三）....................................222

寿阳曲...................................222

秋思（一）.........................222

（二）....................................223

（三）....................................223

（四）....................................223

（五）....................................223

（六）....................................223

（七）....................................224

赵孟頫

后庭花...................................224

11

Wang Shifu

From A Year's End

(I) 53

(II) 53

Teng Bin

Universal Joy 54

Deng Yubin

Chattering Song (I) 55

(II) 55

Ali Xiying

Joy before Palace 56

Feng Zizhen

Song of Parrot (I) 57

(II) 57

Zhu Lianxiu

Song of Long-lived Sun 58

Guan Yunshi

Autumn Swan on Frontier ... 58

Embroidered Red Shoes 59

Falling Mume Blossoms 59

Song of Moon Palace 60

Song of Clear River 61

王实甫

十二月过尧民歌：

别情（一）........................225

（二）........................225

滕宾

普天乐..............................225

邓玉宾

叨叨令：道情（一）......226

（二）........................226

阿里西瑛

殿前欢..............................227

冯子振

鹦鹉曲：山亭逸兴..........227

鹦鹉曲：别意..................227

珠帘秀

寿阳曲..............................228

贯云石

塞鸿秋..............................228

红绣鞋..............................228

落梅风..............................229

蟾宫曲..............................229

清江引..............................229

Zhang Yanghao

Triumphant Song 61

Song of Daffodils 62

Sheep on the Slope 62

Skyward Song 63

Bai Bi

Song of Parrot 64

Zheng Guangzu

Song of Moon Palace (I) 65

(II) 65

Zeng Rui

Hearing the Cuckoo in My Boudoir

(I) 66

(II) 66

(III) 67

Palace Grief (I) 67

(II) 68

(III) 68

(IV) 69

(V) 69

(VI) 70

张养浩

得胜令 230

水仙子 230

山坡羊 230

朝天子 231

白贲

鹦鹉曲 231

郑光祖

蟾宫曲（一）................... 231

（二）............................... 232

曾瑞

骂玉郎过感皇恩采茶歌：

闺中闻杜鹃（一）........... 232

（二）............................... 232

（三）............................... 232

集贤宾（一）................... 233

（二）............................... 233

（三）............................... 233

（四）............................... 233

（五）............................... 234

（六）............................... 234

Sui Jingchen

The Emperor's Home-Coming

(I) 70

(II) 71

(III) 72

(IV) 72

(V) 73

(VI) 73

(VII) 74

(VIII) 74

Zhou Wenzhi

Chattering Song 75

Song of Frontier 75

Qiao Ji

Song of Clear River (I) 76

(II) 76

Sheep on the Slope (I) 77

(II) 77

(III) 78

Song of Flower Seller 78

Leaning on Balustrade(I) ...79

(II) 79

睢景臣

哨遍

（一）.................................234

（二）.................................235

（三）.................................235

（四）.................................235

（五）.................................235

（六）.................................236

（七）.................................236

（八）.................................236

周文质

叨叨令.................................237

塞儿令.................................237

乔吉

清江引：有感....................237

清江引：即景....................238

山坡羊：冬日写怀（一）...238

（二）.................................238

（三）.................................238

卖花声.................................239

凭阑人：春思....................239

凭阑人：小姬....................239

(III) 80
Plucking Laurel Branch (I) .. 80
(II) 81
(III) 82
(IV) 83
Courtyard full of Fragrance:
Song of a fisherman (I) 84
(II) 85
Joy before Palace 86
Red Peach Blossoms 86
Song of Daffodils (I) 87
(II) 87
From Falling Swan (I) 88
(II) 88
Meeting of Good Friends (I) 89
(II) 89
(III) 90
(IV) 90

Liu Shizhong
Joy before Palace 91

Aluwei
Falling Mume Blossoms 91

凭阑人：金陵道中 239
折桂令：毗陵晚眺 240
折桂令：登毗陵永庆阁所见 .. 240
折桂令：客窗清明 240
折桂令：荆溪即事 241
满庭芳：渔父词
（一）............................. 241
（二）............................. 241
殿前欢 242
小桃红 242
水仙子：寻梅 242
水仙子：为友人作 243
雁儿落过得胜令（一）.. 243
（二）............................. 243
集贤宾（一）.................... 244
（二）............................. 244
（三）............................. 244
（四）............................. 244

刘时中
殿前欢 245

阿鲁威
落梅风 245

15

Wang Yuanding
Drunk in Time of Peace 92

Xue Angfu
Autumn Swan on Frontier...92

From Far-flung Southern Sky

(I)..................................93

(II) 93

Wu Hongdao
Golden Canon (I)...............94

(II) 94

Unbroken String (I)............95

(II) 95

Zhao Shanqing
Plucking Laurel Branch 96

Intoxicated in East Wind........97

Blessed Eastern Plain...........97

Ma Qianzhai
Song of Willowy Camp 98

Zhang Kejiu
Man and Moon (I) 99

(II) 100

(III) 101

Drunk in Time of Peace (I).....102

王元鼎
醉太平..................................245

薛昂夫
塞鸿秋..................................246

楚天遥过清江引：送春

（一）..................................246

（二）..................................246

吴弘道
金字经（一）..................246

（二）..................................247

拨不断（一）..................247

（二）..................................247

赵善庆
折桂令..................................248

沉醉东风..................................248

庆东原..................................248

马谦斋
柳营曲..................................249

张可久
人月圆：山中书事...........249

人月圆：春晚次韵...........249

人月圆：春日湖上...........250

醉太平：怀古..................250

(II) 102

Orange and Mume on Brocade
.... 103

Greeting A Fairy Guest 103

Embroidered Red Shoes (I) .. 104

(II) 104

Plane Leaves (I) 105

(II) 105

Plucking Laurel Branch (I) ... 106

(II) 107

(III) 108

(IV) 109

Song of Daffodils 110

Red Peach Blossoms 110

Universal Joy (I) 111

(II) 112

Welcome to Spring (I) 113

(II) 113

Skyward Song 114

Sheep on the Slope 114

Joy before Palace 115

醉太平：感怀 250

锦橙梅
.... 251

迎仙客 251

红绣鞋：宁元帅席上 251

红绣鞋：虎丘道上 251

梧叶儿：湖山夜景 252

梧叶儿：有所思 252

折桂令：西陵送别 252

折桂令：九日 253

折桂令：次韵 253

折桂令：村庵即事 253

水仙子 254

小桃红 254

普天乐：西湖即事 254

普天乐：秋怀 255

喜春来：金华客舍 255

喜春来：永康驿中 255

朝天子 256

山坡羊 256

殿前欢 256

Song of Clear River 116	清江引.............................257
Sunny Sand 116	天净沙.............................257
Leaning on Balustrade 116	凭阑人.............................257
A Sprig of Flowers (I) 117	一枝花（一）..................258
(II) 117	（二）.............................258
(III) 118	（三）.............................258

Xu Zaisi   徐再思

Universal Joy 119	普天乐.............................259
Welcome to Spring...........120	喜春来.............................259
Song of Moon Palace (I)..120	蟾宫曲：江淹寺 259
(II) 121	蟾宫曲：春情..................260
Song of Daffodils (I)........122	水仙子：夜雨 260
(II) 122	水仙子：春情..................260
Man and Moon 123	人月圆.............................261
Skyward Song..................124	朝天子.............................261

Zha Deqing   查德卿

Half and Half 125	一半儿.............................261
Song of Willowy Camp ...125	柳营曲.............................262

Tang Yifu   唐毅夫

A Sprig of Flowers (I) 126	一枝花（一）..................262
(II) 126	（二）.............................262
(III) 128	（三）.............................263

Zhu Tingyu
Sunny Sand 128

Zhang Mingshan
Universal Joy (I) 129

(II) 130

(III) 131

Yang Chaoying
Song of Daffodils 132

Song Fanghu
Sheep on the Slope 133

Song of Clear River 134

Fight of Quails (I) 134

(II) 135

(III) 135

(IV) 136

(V) 136

(VI) 137

Jia Gu
From Drinking Song

(I) 137

(II) 138

Zhou Deqing
Autumn Swan on Frontier ... 138

朱庭玉
天净沙 263

张鸣善
普天乐：咏世 264

普天乐：愁怀 264

普天乐：嘲西席 264

杨朝英
水仙子 265

宋方壶
山坡羊 265

清江引 265

斗鹌鹑（一）................... 266

（二）........................... 266

（三）........................... 266

（四）........................... 266

（五）........................... 267

（六）........................... 267

贾固
醉高歌过红绣鞋：寄金莺儿

（一）........................... 267

（二）........................... 267

周德清
塞鸿秋 268

Courtyard Full of Fragrance ... 139

Plucking Laurel Branch 140

Ban Weizhi

A Sprig of Flowers (I) 141

(II) 142

(III) 143

Wang Yuanheng

Drunk in Time of Peace .. 143

Skyward Song 144

Intoxicated in East Wind ... 145

Ni Zan

Man and Moon 146

Red Peach Blossoms 146

Leaning on Balustrade 147

Song of Daffodils 147

Liu Tingxin

Plucking Laurel Branch ... 148

Song of Daffodils 149

A Sprig of Flowers 151

Tang Shi

Minor Frontier

(I) 151

(II) 152

满庭芳 268

折桂令 268

班惟志

一枝花（一）..................... 269

（二）................................ 269

（三）................................ 269

汪元亨

醉太平 270

朝天子 270

沉醉东风 270

倪瓒

人月圆 271

小桃红 271

凭阑人 271

水仙子 271

刘庭信

折桂令 272

水仙子 272

一枝花 273

汤式

小梁州：

九日渡江（一）............. 273

（二）................................ 273

Song of Celestial Fragrance...153

Lan Chufang

Four Pieces of Jade (I) 154

(II) 154

Zhong Sicheng

Intoxicated in Time of Peace

(I)................................155

(II)...............................155

Qian Lin

Whistling Around (I) 156

(II) 157

(III) 157

(IV) 158

(V) 158

(VI) 159

(VII) 159

(VIII) 160

(IX) 160

(X) 161

(XI) 161

(XII) 162

天香引.............................274

兰楚芳

四块玉：风情（一）.......274

（二）............................275

钟嗣成

醉太平：落魄

（一）................................ 275

（二）...............................275

钱霖

哨遍（一）........................276

（二）..............................276

（三）..............................276

（四）..............................277

（五）..............................277

（六）..............................277

（七）.............................. 277

（八）.............................. 278

（九）.............................. 278

（十）..............................278

（十一）........................ 278

（十二）........................ 279

Sun Zhouqing
Song of the Moon Palace ... 162

Cao De
Blessed Eastern Plain 163

Zhen Shi
Thrice Drunk and Sobered 164

Wu Xiyi
Sunny Sand 164

Song of the Clear River ... 165

Song of Long-lived Sun ... 165

Cheng Jingchu
Drunk in Time of Peace 166

Anonymous
Song of Daffodils (I) 167

(II) 167

(III) 168

Plucking Laurel Branch (I) ... 169

(II) 170

Autumn Swan on Frontier

(I) 171

(II) 171

Plane Leaves (I) 172

(II) 172

孙周卿
蟾宫曲 279

曹德
庆东原 279

真氏
解三酲 280

吴西逸
天净沙 280

清江引 280

寿阳曲 280

程景初
醉太平 281

无名氏
水仙子（一）..................... 281

（二）............................. 281

（三）............................. 282

折桂令（一）..................... 282

（二）............................. 282

塞鸿秋
（一）............................. 283

（二）............................. 283

梧叶儿（一）..................... 283

（二）............................. 284

Changes of Tunes (I) 173	四换头（一）.................... 284
(II) 173	（二）............................. 284
Embroidered Red Shoes (I).... 174	红绣鞋（一）.................... 285
(II) 174	（二）............................. 285
(III) 175	（三）............................. 285
(IV) 175	（四）............................. 285
Celebration of Imperial Reign 176	庆宣和 286
Intoxicated in East Wind (I) 176	沉醉东风 （一）............................. 286
(II) 177	（二）............................. 286
Song of Frontier 177	塞儿令 287
Ascending the Attic 178	上小楼 287
Parasite Grass 178	寄生草 287
From Happy Three (I) 179	快活三过朝天子四换头 （一）............................. 288
(II) 179	（二）............................. 288
(III) 180	（三）............................. 288
Reading Golden Classics.... 180	阅金经 288
Universal Joy 181	普天乐 289
From Falling Swan (I)....... 181	雁儿落过得胜令（一）.. 289
(II) 182	（二）............................. 289

Chattering Song (I) 182	叨叨令（一）...................290
(II) 183	（二）...............................290
(III) 183	（三）...............................290
The Four Gates Visited (I)....184	游四门（一）...................291
(II) 184	（二）...............................291
Thrice in Jade Pavilion.....185	三番玉楼人.......................291
Skyward Song..................186	朝天子...............................292
Embroidered Red Shoes ..187	红绣鞋...............................292
Welcome to Spring..........187	喜春来...............................292
From Happy Three	快活三过朝天子四换头：
(I)..................................188	忆别（一）.......................293
(II) 188	（二）...............................293
(III) 189	（三）...............................293
From Blaming My Gallant	骂玉郎过感皇恩采茶歌
(I)..................................189	（一）...............................294
(II) 190	（二）...............................294
(III) 190	（三）...............................294

CLASSICAL CHINESE POETRY AND PROSE

300 YUAN SONGS

TRANSLATED BY XU YUANCHONG

China Intercontinental Press   Zhonghua Book Company

Preface

How can we know the cultural level of a nation? We may see how many masterpieces her people has created for mankind. Tang poetry, Song lyrics and Yuan songs are masterpieces created by the Chinese people from the seventh to the fourteenth centuries. Poetry is the voice of the mind, As Confucius said, "poetry serves to inspire, to reflect, to communicate and to criticize," we may say to voice what is in the mind is to inspire others, to reflect reality, to communicate with people and to criticize the times. In Tang poetry, Song lyrics and Yuan songs we can find inspiration to the mind, reflections of the times, communion with Heaven above and criticism on evils below. For instance, in Tang poetry we can see Li Bai's communion with nature and man in his romanticism, Du Fu's reflections of the people's misery in his classicism, Bai juyi's criticism of the evils of the times in his realism, and Li Shangyin's inspiration to the mind in his symbolism, which may be said to be earlier than these literary trends in the west by a thousand years. In Song lyrics we can find lyricism in Liu Yong, rationalism in Su Dongpo, colloquialism in Li Qingzhao and satirism in Xin Qiji. On the one hand, both Tang and Song poets are successors to ancient literary tradition crystallized in the *Book of Poetry* compiled by Confucius; on the other, they have exercised great influence on Yuan songs.

The Tang and Song dynasties are the golden ages in Chinese history. During these six hundred years the Chinese empire was the most prosperous, most developed, most civilized country in the world, while the west was under the reign of the Dark Ages. But during the

Yuan Dynasty, the Mongols came from the north to conquer the central plain. They became the rulers and oppressed the southern people. The Mongols might kill Southerners without reason and without being punished. The conquered intellectuals sank so low in their social position that they were classified even under prostitutes and only above beggars. These phenomena are reflected in songs. For example, Zhong Sicheng sang of the beggar:

> I ask if there's a charitable miss
> Who would give me a hearty meal.

and of a poor scholar:

> I would repair an old brick-kiln with clay
> And open a school for beggars by day.
> I'll put on a black hat half outworn
> And a yellow cloak half torn.

And Zhen Shi sang of a prostitute:

> It is my duty to please men by my beauty,
> But behind them my tears fall in streams.

Here we see the realism of Tang poets extended more deeply to the lower class of people.

What could intellectuals do under such oppression but voice their discontent and hatred in songs? For example, an anonymous poet wrote the following stanza:

> Those who can't read are powerful,
> Those who can't write pass wealthy days,
> The ignorant may win high praise.
> Is it not Heaven's care to be just and fair?

How can He not know the good from the fool?

Or the intellectual could only try to find a secluded place and live a hermetic life, as Feng Zizhen wrote in his *Song of Parrot*:

> Pointing to clouds and hills before my door,
> I need not pay for the scene I adore.

They tried to enjoy the beauty of nature as described by Qiao Ji in his *Song of Fisherman*:

> None could forbid running water or floating cloud;
> I'm better than the lord of woods or mountains proud.
> The rainbow clouds steeped in cold waves look like brocades;
> The autumn moon like molten gold on the sea fades.

But nature was not always beautiful, and poets might come in face of frowning peaks which would remind them of people's woe as described by Zhang Yanghao:

> Peaks like brows knit,
>
> Angry waves split.
>
> The ancient palaces, hall on hall,
> Are turned to dust, one and all.
>
> Before my eyes,
>
> The empire's rise
>
> Is people's woe;
>
> The empire's fall
>
> Is also people's woe.

Some poets tried to escape from reality by reviving the memory of ancient heroes, as is found in Zhou Deqing's *Tomb of General Yue Fei*:

> By word and sword he tried

> To rebuild the royal temple's fame,
> And left in history an undying name.
>   But envied by traitors before he had won,
> He was treacherously slain,
> Leaving unrecovered the lost Central Plain,
> And Northern royal tombs not visited again.
>   His work undone,
> The dreary wind and drizzling rain
> Are weeping for the General in vain.

In Yuan songs we can find Tang heroism degenerate into pessimism, Song rationalism into passivism, their lyricism popularized, but their criticism continued and colloquialism developed.

So far as the form is concerned, the Yuan songs admit more freely the use of everyday colloquial speech, the idiom and the slang of common people. For example, we may read Zhang Kejiu's *A Wife Bored*:

> Her boudoir closed, she's deep in vernal sleep.
>   Willow down flies,
>   Her young maid cries:
>   "Lo! what auspicious snow!"
> It wakes her from the dream of her love she will keep.
>   "Who?
>   What a bore! Oh!
>   It is you."

Here we see Li Qingzhao's colloquialism vulgarized. In Li's lyric we only find the following:

> "Do you not know

The red should languish and the green must grow?"

Besides, extra words are used in Yuan songs in addition to what is required by the melody. For instance, we may read Xu Zaisi's *Song of Daffodils*:

> I am as lovesick as I'm full of care;
> We long for each other here and there.
> Ten years of courting give me as much joy as pain;
> Our life is chequered with loss as well as gain.
> There is not half a thing which brings me not half shame,
> In autumn late I regret autumn flame;
> In springtime fine I complain I'm sick of spring wine.
> All my life long is nothing but a love song.

Xu Zaisi's song consists of eight lines and only forty-eight words, but Liu Tingxin's *Song of Daffodils* is enlarged to twenty-nine lines and one hundred words, that is to say, there are fifty-two extra words in the latter, of which I only cite the first four lines as example:

> Oh, deep regret
> On regret deep
> I can't forget!
> At dusk it overwhelms my bower and I weep.

Just read the first two lines, and you will find extra words used in repetition, but they are not repeated in vain for they enhance the emotion the poet tries to express.

Parallelism is an important feature in Tang and Song poetry. For instance, we may read Du Fu's wellknown balanced couplet:

> The boundless forest sheds its leaves shower by shower;

The endless river rolls its waves hour after hour.

In Yuan songs, the couplet has developed into "triplet", that is to say, three balanced lines of verse equal in length and with thyme. For example, we may read a "triplet" taken from Ma Zhiyuan's song sequence:

> See ants surround their prey in flood,
> Bees gather honey pellmell,
> And flies hasten to suck blood.

Yuan songs may be classified into three types, namely, short song, song sequence and dramatic song. A short song consists of only one stanza; a song sequence of more than two or three. For instance, Du Renjie's *Playing the Child* consists of seven stanzas and its theme *A Peasant Knows Not the Theatre* is realistic as Bai Juyi's poem. Guan Hanqing's *A Sprig of Flowers* consists of four stanzas and its theme *Don't say I'm Old* is critical as Xin Qiji's lyric. Ma Zhiyuan's *Night-Sailing Boat* consists of seven stanzas and its theme is rational as Su Shi's poetry. Zeng Rui's *Meeting of Good Friends* consists of six stanzas and its theme *Palace Grief* is lyrical as Liu Yong's verse. Ju Jingchen's *Whistling Around* consists of eight stanzas and its theme *The Emperor's Home-Coming* is satirical. Qiao Ji's *Parting under Willows Recalled*, Zhang Kejiu's *Return from the Lake* and Song Fanghu's *Fight of Quails* are lyrical. Qian Lin's *Whistling Around* consists of twelve stanzas and its theme *The Miser* is critical. Thus we see how Yuan poets have inherited from Tang poetry and Song lyrics and developed according to the circumstances. What achieves higher development is the dramatic song as represented by Wang Shifu's *Romance of the Western Bower*, which is too long to be included in this collection.

In short, we may say Yuan poets have inherited the poetic tradition to inspire, reflect, communicate and criticize and developed in accordance with the times, popularied poetry, liberalized versification and diversified the metrical forms. Thus they have paved the way for modern vernacular Chinese literature.

Xu Yuanchong
February 14, 2004

Yuan Haowen

TUNE: MAN AND MOON
MOVING TO MY MOTHER'S EAST GARDEN

(I)

Hill on hill keeps apart the vanity fair
From this village of bumper year.
I move house to come near
The window-enframed distant hill
And the pine-trees behind the windowsill.

I'll leave the woods and fields to the care
Of my children dear
So that I may do what I will.
Awake, I'll enjoy the moon so bright;
Drunk, the refreshing breeze so light.

(II)

In Royal Temple there are thousands of peach trees,
Whence fallen blooms in vain with water flow.
Do not ask, please,
If water is not clear,
Or cows will come or horses go.

What matters if the minister was ill,
And his friend shed tear on tear!
What can I do but drink my fill?
How many splendid houses of olden days appear
Fallen to ruins in the hill!

TUNE: MINOR SACRED MUSIC
SUDDEN SHOWER BEATING ON NEW LOTUS LEAVES

(I)

Green leaves casting deep shade
Over pavilions and bowers by the pool
Bring a delightful cool.
The pomegranates in early flower
Look like frowning red brocade.
Young swallows chirp and orioles warble their song
While cicadas on high willow trees trill along,
A sudden shower
With raindrops like pearls or dew
Beats on lotus leaves new.

(II)

How many people can live to a hundred years?
Do not let golden hours and fine scenery
Slip away!
Our poor destiny
Cannot be turned another way.
It's better to invite friends and enjoy with peers
Good wine and songs we sing low.
Be tipsy while we may,
And let sun and moon come and go
Like shuttles to and fro!

Yang Guo

TUNE: RED PEACH BLOSSOMS
THE LOTUS GATHERER

(I)

The dimming moon o'er mist-veiled town and water looms.

The beauty in orchid boat sings her dream.

I oft remember our meeting on silk-washing stream.

Now severed by three rivers long,

In vain through clouds into the azure sky I gaze.

Smiling, the beauty says,

"Our hearts are like the lotus blooms:

Their root may snap, their fibres join like my song."

(II)

Having gathered the lotus on the lake, she rows

On homeward way, her green skirt ripples when wind blows.

A song of pipa brings down tear on tear;

In vain she waits for her lord to appear.

Now lotus blooms all faded, he is not in sight,

How many lovebirds red and egrets white

She sees in the cool evening sky!

Nowhere but in pairs will they fly.

Liu Bingzhong

Dried Lotus Leaves

(I)

Lotus leaves dried
In color turned from green to grey,
Old stems in the wind sway.
With fragrance lost, they are in yellow dyed.
Last night frost chilled their dream.
They look now lonely on the autumn stream.

(II)

Dried lotus leaves,
Whose color grieves,
Can't bear the bite of hoary frost.
On autumn waves they're lost
With their stems broken.
The palace maids awoken
Sing songs of lotus gathered on the stream,
Whose prime is passed in dream.

(III)

Southern Peak high,
Northern Peak high,
The Cave of Rainbow Clouds utter a dreary sigh.
The Song Emperor High
In vain has now gone by.
On Southern Hills the wineshop streamers fly
Still as of yore,
But the thriving days of Song are no more.

Du Renjie

TUNE: PLAYING THE CHILD
A PEASANT KNOWS NOT THE THEATRE

(I)

People live happy when in time blows wind and falls rain,
But as we peasants none's so cheerful and gay
In bumper year of mulberry and grain
When no official disturbs us everyday.
My vow fulfilled, I should perform the rural rite,
So I go downtown to buy incense and candles bright.
As I pass by the fair,
I see colored ads hanging there.
Nowhere have I seen a more noisy crowd, nowhere!

(II) THE LAST BUT SIX

I see a man keep the gate open with one hand,
Crying loud: "Come in please, please!
Late, you'll find the house full and nowhere to sit but stand.
First, actors will perform *the Moon and Breeze*,
And then the play of an actor wellknown to this land.
It's easy to find a place to enjoy and pause,
But hard to win your hearty applause."

(III) THE LAST BUT FIVE

I pay two hundred coins and I'm let in.

I enter, mount a wooden slope and hear a din.

I see an amphitheatre with seats in tier.

Looking up, I see a tower like stage appear;

Looking down, I find the crowd like a whirlpool,

And women musicians sitting on the stool.

It is not a sacred procession long.

Why do I hear without cease drum and gong?

(IV) THE LAST BUT FOUR

For several rounds a maiden comes forth and back,

Then she leads a group of four from the rear.

Among them there's a villain clown,

Whose head is wrapped in a hood black,

With a brush on the ear;

Whose face with lime is white,

Streaked with paint black as night.

What will he do?

From top to toe,

He wears a motley gown.

(V) THE LAST BUT THREE

He reads some verse

And sings some song,

There's nothing wrong.

Who knows which's better and which worse?

I only remember many words sweet.

What at the end is said?

He bends his head and keeps close his feet.

After the prelude, the melodrama will be played.

(VI) THE LAST BUT TWO

One actor plays the role of grandpa old,

Another acts the waiter of a wine shop.

They walk and talk of life,

And at the central place they stop,

Seeing a young woman standing under the screen.

The grandpa covets her as wife,

And asks the waiter to be go-between,

How much grain, rice, peas and wheat

She wants as dowry and how many feet

Of cloth, silk, satin and brocade, all told.

(VII) THE LAST BUT ONE

Told to go forward, ay!

The grandpa dare not backward go.

Told to raise his foot high,

He dare not put it low.

He turns back and forth as he is led,

Anxious at heart, he starts

And breaks the leather-wrapped hammer into two parts,

I mistake it for a broken head,

And fear they'll go to court after,

But unexpectedly I hear them burst in laughter.

(VIII) THE LAST SONG OR EPILOGUE

Hard pressed to pass water, I make for the door.

Though I try to hold it back so as to see more.

But how can I be set free?

I am afraid these sons of bitch will laugh at me.

Wang Heqing

TUNE: A DRINKER'S SKY
SONG OF A HUGE BUTTERFLY

Breaking a philosopher's dream,
He flaps his wings and rides on the east wind in flight.
He gathers all the honey from the flowers
In three hundred well-known gardens and bowers.
Don't say the lover of beauty and breeze
Has scared away all honey-seeking bees!
Flapping his fan-like wings so light,
He blows the flower-seller off across the stream.

TUNE: HALF AND HALF
PARTING GRIEF

(I)

When I receive his letter, my tears rain;
I am afraid to open it, for again and again
He said he'd come back, but in vain.
How could I not grow thin and my grief be appeased?
When one half has decreased, the other has increased.

(II)

I take his letter near at hand,
And read it by lamplight carefully.
He wrote carelessly these two lines or three,
Which I am anxious to understand.
Half of his letter is torn apart,
Another half burns my heart.

(III)

My golden robe turns loose since my love from me parted;
My powdered face and jade like skin look broken-hearted.
Tears dripping drop by drop only known to my sleeves, I
Wait for him with a sigh,
My sleeves are half wet and half dry.

He Xicun

Tune: Red Peach Blossoms
(I) Lantern Lights on the River

Thousands of lanterns run riot on vernal shore,
Light overspreads for miles and miles.
Wonderful dancing phoenixes and dragons soar
Into the lovely night.
Out of the waves emerge three fairy isles.
See incense waft in flight;
Hear music on flute played!
They fly up around the tower of jade.

Tune: Red Peach Blossoms
(II) River Bay at Dusk

The clear bay is locked in clouds green-dyed,
Fragrance spreads to east and west riverside.
Only nine-tenths of taxes need be paid this year.
How joyful people appear!
At the ferry they buy fresh fowls and fishes
To make plentiful dishes.
Their joy reaches its prime,
All forget the hard time.

Tune: Red Peach Blossoms
(III) Mid-Spring

Since apricots bloomed, the weather drear
Has disappointed the sightseer.
Blooms fall like red snow over the fragrant way.
I ask the oriole where is spring;
It answers not and the wind dies away.
Hear the young songstress sing
When all are still in the cool night!
Only she sings for the old drinker out of sight.

Shang Ting

Tune: Song of Princess Pan

Shivering with fright
In moonlight and starlight,
I stand long by the window dim,
Waiting for him.
Suddenly outdoor footsteps I seem to hear:
O it must be my dear.
But how again I shiver
To find in the wind only the trellis quiver.

Hu Zhiyu

TUNE: INTOXICATED IN EAST WIND
FISHERMAN AND WOODCUTTER

A fisherman is content with a basketful of fishes;
A woodcutter with a bundle of firewood he wishes.
One smiles on shouldering his fishing rod and line;
The other, with brows unknit, puts back his ax fine.
By chance they meet beside the fountain.
Though illiterate, they know much in the mountain.
Now and then they burst into laughter,
When they talk about the days before and after.

Bo Yan

TUNE: WELCOME TO SPRING

Adorned with gold fish and belt of jade,
I button my robe of brocade,
Under black canopy and banners red,
Of the five highest lords I'm at the head.
The land is ruled at the tip of my pen.
What pride over all men!
I bear my share of the imperial care.

Wang Yun

Tune: Joy of Calm Lake
Autumn Festival at Emperor Yao's Temple

The incense on the altar fades
And crows disperse into the glades.
Wine cup in hand and bumper harvest in view,
I hear strings rumbling low and high
Mingle with cheerful cry.
Beyond Labor Pavilion hills look like pictures fair.
At dawn the western hills exhale fresh air.
Why should I envy Southern Mountain hue?

Lu Zhi

Tune: Higher and Higher
Written on the Temple Wall on Lake Dongting

After the rain clouds clear away;
Over the lake the moon sheds its ray.
The waves are calmed when the wind light
Blows on my leaflike boat at midnight.
In my heart deep,
Of my past life I dream.
I'll go far on the stream;
Depressed in the lonely boat, I get a short sleep.

TUNE: INTOXICATED IN EAST WIND
(I) AUTUMN

The frowning cliff thrusts out a bending ancient pine;
With lonely swan fly rainbow clouds on the decline.
Surrounded by endless hill on hill,
On boundless water I gaze my fill.
The western breeze spreads autumn air in wide, wide skies.
The shadow of my cloudlike sail hangs low at moonrise.
My boat seems to float in the picture of two streams.

TUNE: INTOXICATED IN EAST WIND
(II) RURAL LIFE

Having just left green hills and water blue,
I come to thatched cots with fence of bamboo.
By the roadside wild flowers blow;
In the trough I see home brew flow,
I eat till drunk, I stagger along.
The lad won't care if I am wrong
To wear yellow flowers on my white hair.

TUNE: INTOXICATED IN EAST WIND
(III) SPRING

Bees gather honey from lingering flowers;

Swallows build nest with clay wet with showers.

Willow down wafts like snow white,

Like rosy rain peach petals in flight.

The cuckoos sing the parting spring.

Though I write new verse when you part,

How can I cure you of your lovesick heart!

TUNE: SONG OF MOON PALACE
(I) AT A FEAST IN THE RIVER TOWN

In river town songs are sung with the flowing breeze.

The rain has passed over plain and hill,

The western tower steeped in moonbeams.

How many years are gone with ease?

My life old and new drunk away in dreams,

The sixth moon foretells an autumn cool.

My wine cup filled by lutist beautiful,

Crimson curtain uprolled, I hear songs of frontier.

How can I not linger still?
Before me cloud-veiled trees shiver
Under the endless Heaven's River.

TUNE: SONG OF MOON PALACE
(II) WRITTEN FOR MY FAIR SONGSTRESS WHILE DRUNK

Who sends you, my fair songstress, to my boat?

I love you come like breeze into the wood with ease.

Beyond the cloud your songs float,

I see your cloudlike hair

And hear your icy strings spread rain in the air,

In which I find a genius mind.

The south wind blows from green woods into evening sky.

Your songs would make warbling orioles feel shy.

When guests leave the post, I seem to be lost.

Awake from drunken dream,

I write this on the stream.

TUNE: JOY BEFORE PALACE
WINE

Deep drunk,

In a gourd of spring hue I'm sunk.

A gourd of wine weighs down the tip of tree,

My page follows me.

My gourd is dried,

I'm still in spirits high.

Who will take a drink by my side?

A belt of green hills will not say goodbye.

On the wind I ride.

Who is riding, the wind or I?

Chen Cao'an

TUNE: SHEEP ON THE SLOPE
O WORLD!

At dawn cock crows;

At dusk caw crows,

Who to vanity fair is not eager to go?

Long long the way;

Far far the stream.

Only in the capital can you fulfil your dream.

Tomorrow old will grow the youth of today.

The hills are as green as before,

But the prime of youth is no more.

Guan Hanqing

TUNE: SONG OF WHITE CRANE

Incense in golden censer burned,
I stand in red bower unconcerned.
The moon atop the willow tree,
At dusk my lover trysts with me.

TUNE: FOUR PIECES OF JADE
PARTING GRIEF

Since you are gone,
For you I long.
When will my yearning come to end?
I lean on rails, caressed by snow-like willow down.
The stream you went along
At hillside takes a bend.
It's screened from view
Together with you.

TUNE: FOUR PIECES OF JADE
LIFE OF EASY LEISURE

(I)

Halt running horse and bind
Ape-like whimsical mind!
Leap out of a world which raves with dust and waves!
Wake up from noonday dream of glory vain!
Get rid of fame and gain!
Take a rest in your nest of pleasure
And enjoy your leisure!

(II)

Having tilled the southern field, I
At the foot of eastern hill lie.
I've known the world and its ways,
And ponder at leisure the past days.
O wise is he
And foolish me!
What should I contend to be?

TUNE: INTOXICATED IN EAST WIND
FAREWELL SONG

We stand so near yet we'll be poles apart soon;

In a moment flowers will fall and wane the moon.

We hold in hand the farewell cup,

In our eyes tears well up.

I have just said, "Take care to keep fit!"

How painful is it

To tear myself away!

I can only say, "Go your way for the bright day!"

TUNE: SONG OF GREAT VIRTUE
(I)

In the Fair's Village lingering,

I seek the beauty of last spring.

I wonder if the peach blossoms laugh at me.

Who will tell me where is she?

I cannot force myself to write a verse.

My broken heart turns out worse.

In flowers' shade I have no one to ask but wait;

I only hear a dog bark at the wicket gate.

(II)

The wind soughs hour after hour;
The rain falls shower by shower.
Even the Sleeping God cannot fall asleep.
Regret and sorrow hurt me deep,
My tears drip drop by drop,
After cicadas trill crickets chirp without stop.
It further grieves
To hear rain drizzle on banana leaves.

TUNE: GREEN JADE FLUTE

(I)

With zither on my knees,
I'm moved to think of my far-off dear.
My fingers play with ease
On zither strings a music clear.
Before my window screen the moon is bright;
Beyond the balustrade fresh is the night.
My touches light
Would make the poets' verve freer.
O Hear!
From water clock there comes no sound;
Silence begins to reign all around.

(II)

At the banquet, before a cup of wine,

Beside the flowers, beneath the willow,

For years I've sung and you've written verse fine.

But we've no chance to share the quilt and pillow.

What before others dare I say?

I can only in my heart pray.

Though our love firm remain,

Yet day by day we meet in vain.

Which day,

O Heaven, in our life

Can we be man and wife?

TUNE: A SPRIG OF FLOWERS
(I) DON'T SAY I'M OLD

I pluck flower on flower over the wall,
And break off branch on branch of willow tree.
The red pistil of the flower is tender;
The green twigs of the willow are slender.
A gallant like me
Will gather flowers and break off branches till I see
Withered leaves and flowers fall.
I have been picking them half my life;
I'll love and sleep with them as with a wife.

(II) TUNE: THE FRONTIER

I am the leading gallant under the sky,
And the most dissolute lover on earth.
I wish no face should lose its rosy dye.
I'd lead among flowers a life of mirth,
And drown my sorrow in wine;
I'd drink tea, paint bamboos fine,
Gamble on horse-race and in lottery.
There is no music but I can play a part.

How could sorrow come into my heart?
Who is in my company
But the lutist leaning on silver screen
And playing on silver lute in silver bower;
Hand in hand and side by side, the fairy queen
Going up with me to the jade tower;
The songstress adorned with golden hairpin,
Golden cup in hand, singing of golden dress and flower?
You say I'm old and should retire,
But in gallantry I'm going up higher and higher.
Growing more clever for ever and ever,
I'm winner in the camp of flowers,
Loafing from place to place, in golden bowers.

(III) TUNE: THE INTERLUDE

The young gallants are new-born bucks in chase of does,

Coming out of the burrows in the mound,

And running for the first time on hunting ground.

I'm an old pheasant with feather grey,

Having escaped from traps and nets on the way,

And running like a steed

At fullest speed,

Nearly hit by spearheads and arrows from hidden bows,

Now I've reached middle age and known so many things,

How could I waste more autumns and springs?

(IV) TUNE: EPILOGUE

I'm a resounding copper pea
Which could not be
Hammered out, cooked, fried or stewed.
How can you young gallants penetrate into me
Like a manifold harness which cannot be
Hoed up or cut down,
Slowly rid of or quickly hewed?
I have enjoyed in royal garden the moonshine,
In the east capital good wine,
And peony flowers in the west,
And plucked a twig from my lover's breast.
I'm good at poetry
And at calligraphy;
I can play on the string
And draw a picture of bamboo,
I can also sing
The songs of partridge too.
With hands hanging down I can dance,
In hunting I can advance,

I know how to play football and chess,
And I gamble by chance.
You may knock my teeth down
Or my mouth wry,
Even if you break
My leg and hand,
Though disabled am I,
Still firm I'll stand,
Unless
The Satanic Majesty
Or the demons come to summon me.
Even one-third of my soul goes to the hell
And two-thirds sink into the infernal well,
O Heaven, only then
Will I not go on the dark willowy lane.

Bai Pu

TUNE: PARASITE GRASS
DRINKING

What ails when I'm drunk long?
When I don't wake, what's wrong?
Let undying fame and glory be drowned in wine!
Forget the ups and downs of days gone by!
Bury in songs ambitions rainbow-high!
The unsuccessful laugh at Qu Yuan in water sunk,
While connoisseurs approve Tao Qian in wine drunk.

TUNE: SONG OF SPRING
FOR MY LOVE

I take up my pen light stained with tears to write
My heart-felt grief and then T fold the paper white.
Alas! unused to lasting longing for a mate,
It takes me such a long, long time to wait
For your vain promise of a date.

TUNE: SUNNY SAND
(I) SPRING

The sun and gentle breeze warm hills in spring,

The curtained bower girt with balustrade.

Among the willows in the garden hangs the swing.

The swallows dance and orioles sing

On running stream under the bridge fallen reds fade.

(II) SUMMER

Waves rise when clouds clear away with rain fleet;

By tower high water is cold and melon sweet.

Green willow leaves shade painted eaves.

On bamboo mat in curtained bed, she's fair as jade,

In silken dress with a fan of brocade.

(III) AUTUMN

At sunset over lonely village rainbow clouds glow;
Over mist-veiled old trees flies a cold crow.
The shadow of a dot of swan in flight
Over green hills and bluish rills
Sees leaves red, flowers yellow and dewy grass white.

(IV) WINTER

A dreary horn blows in watch-tower on city wall;
The crescent moon sheds twilight into half the hall;
The waterside and hillside are covered with snow.
A bamboo-fenced cottage only
Stands in the village lonely,
Where with a wreath of smoke wafts a cold crow.

TUNE: INTOXICATED IN EAST WIND
FISHERMAN

The rivershore overgrown with yellow reed,
The ferry decorated with white duckweed,
The bank is shaded by willows green and the beach head
Adorned with knotweed red.
Although I have no life-long friends,
My companions conceive no evil ends.
The autumn river is dotted with gulls and herons white.
I look down on the lords proud of their might.
A fisherman old, I fish in mist and water cold.

Yao Sui

TUNE: DRINKING SONG
REFLECTION

I sigh after ten years with books and sword.
The lutist's song is a promise without word.
I leave the river town when the moon shines bright,
Afraid to hear rain in orchid boat at night.

TUNE: LEANING ON BALUSTRADE
THE WINTER GARMENT

If I send winter garment to thee,
Thou wilt not come to the household.
If I do not, thou wilt feel cold.
It is hard to decide for me
If I should send it to thee.

Yu Tianxi

TUNE: FROM FALLING SWAN TO TRIUMPHANT SONG
(I) TUNE: FALLING SWAN

Let my black hair turn grey!
I'll pillow my head on white stone till its decay.
I turn my head: the setting sun reddens the sky;
Verdant hills look serene to the eye.

(II) TUNE: TRIUMPHANT SONG

Peak on peak stands like emerald;
Cloud on cloud locks the evening cold.
Gaze on the charming vernal plain
And sun-lit hills after the rain!
O brighten up
And fill to the brim with golden wine the jade cup!
Deep in the hill,
It's hard for us to meet, so lets enjoy our fill!

Liu Minzhong

TUNE: VARNISHED BLACK BOW
Written at Random in the Village

Wearing long hood and large collar in my cot,
I'm called a rude fellow by those who know me not.
My wicket gate closed to bamboos green and sand white,
I listen to the rain throughout the autumn night.
Pondering at leisure gain and loss, weal and woe,
I see the past like running water eastward flow.
Even if my portrait should in high tower remain,
Is it the end of glory I try to attain?

Ma Zhiyuan

Tune: Four Pieces of Jade
(I) On River Xunyang

When we two part,

The autumn river is cold.

The lutist's song would break our heart.

Don't you know Poet Bai of old

Who listened to the lute with heart-break?

The moon's as bright;

We're drunken quite,

But soon we wake.

Tune: Four Pieces of Jade
(II) O World!

Grey turns my hair

Past middle age.

Why should I be busy about worldly affair?

I've seen through fame and shame as a sage.

I'd till in vernal breeze two acres of land;

Far from the world's ups and downs I would stand.

What a great pleasure

To live at leisure!

TUNE: SUNNY SAND
AUTUMN THOUGHTS

Over old trees wreathed with rotten vines fly crows;

Under a small bridge beside a cot a stream flows;

On ancient road in western breeze a lean horse goes.

Westwards declines the setting sun.

Far, far from home is the heart-broken one.

TUNE: SONG OF CLEAR RIVER
RURAL PLEASURE
(I)

Green straw cloak and violet silken gown,

Which is up? Which is down?

Neither will do. Even a fisherman

Should avoid perilous waves if he can.

I'd seek a safe place as I please

To sit with ease.

(II)

Who'd come to my hermitage amid the trees?

My only guest is the fresh breeze.

Living by the fountain,

I'm minister in the mountain.

I do not care for worldly affair.

Why should I strive to enter the vanity fair?

TUNE: SONG OF LONG-LIVED SUN
(I) THE SUN-LIT MIST-VEILED MOUNTAIN

By blooming village-side,

West of the shop of wine,

Rainbow clouds after rain brighten the sky far and wide.

The surrounding hills steeped in sinking sunshine,

The embroidered screen is again paved with emerald green.

(II) THE RETURNING SAILS

The sun sinks behind the hill,

The wineshop's streamer's still.

Two or three fishing boats have not yet come ashore.

Fallen petals sweeten water before the door.

By the end of the day

Fish-sellers disperse on homeward way.

(III) NIGHT RAIN ON THE RIVER

Dim fishers' lanternlight,

I wake up from my dream.

The rain drips drop by drop to break my heart.

My lonely boat is far from home deep in the night.

It rains as tears which stream

Down from the eyes of those who part.

TUNE: SONG OF LONG-LIVED SUN

Since thou left me,

I have received no word from thee.

Such unkindness has injured me.

I complain to whoever appears.

I don't believe it won't assail thy ears.

AUTUMN THOUGHTS

(I) TUNE: NIGHT-SAILING BOAT

Like a dream pass a hundred years of light and shade;

Turning my head, I sigh for days gone by.

Spring comes today, tomorrow flowers fade.

Drink the cup dry

Before lamplight goes out at dead of night!

(II) TUNE: THE ARBOR

I think of ancient palaces, alas!

They become pastures covered with withered grass.

The fishermen's gossip they are aliments,

Crisscrossed with ruined tombs and broken monuments,

On which dragons and snakes are blent.

(III) TUNE: CELEBRATION OF THE REIGN

I find fox's traces and hare's holes.

Where are the ancient heroes' souls?

Like a tripod's broken legs the three states are not strong.

To which succeeding dynasty did the empire belong?

(IV) Tune: Falling Mume Blossoms

No matter how rich you may be,
Don't live in luxury!
O happy days and nights cannot forever last.
No matter how hard a miser's heart may be,
The breezy moonlit days will soon be past.

(V) Tune: The Wind Through Pines

The setting sun goes west before the eye
As quickly as the carriage rolling down the height.
Don't let your hair in the mirror turn snow-white!
Go to bed and say to your shoes goodbye!
Don't laugh at the cuckoo occupying the magpie's nest!
Play the fool like a gourd and take your rest!

(VI) TUNE: UNBROKEN STRING

In the vanity fair

There is nor right nor wrong.

No dust is raised before my door all the day long,

The eaves of my roof is shaded by trees green,

My broken wall seems crowned with hills like a screen.

What's more, I've my bamboo-fenced cot in evening air.

(VII) TUNE: FEAST AT FAREWELL PAVILION

When crickets sing,

I can sleep well.

At cockcrow everything

Begins to stir up.

When will end the strife

For fame and gain?

See ants surround their prey in flood,

Bees gather honey pellmell,

And flies hasten to suck blood.

I would retire to the green plain

Or at the foot of White Lotus Hill.

I love, when autumn is chill,

To pluck golden flowers inpearled with dew,

To eat frost-proof crabs with you,

And to burn red leaves to heat wine.

How many cups can we drink in our life?

How many can we enjoy mountain-climbing days fine?

I ask my lad to tell any guest

That I am taking my rest

At my eastern hedge with my wine cup!

Zhao Mengfu

Tune: Backyard Flowers
Autumn Thoughts

On the clear stream she rows a leaf-like boat,

Lotus blooms spread autumn hue to the shore.

Who is gathering lotus seed, at dusk afloat?

She startles gulls with her folklore.

From gloomy clouds grief is shed,

Wind and rain overspread,

She goes back with a lotus leaf over her head.

Wang Shifu

From a Year's End to Folklore
Parting Grief
(I) Tune: A Year's End

Since we parted, far-flung hills disappear with you.
How can I bear to see the rippling stream anew,
And wave on wave of willow catkin's wafting trace,
And peach blossom's drunken face before my face?
The fragrant breeze invades my bower now and then;
Evening rain falls on my closed door again and again.

(II) Tune: Folklore

The dim twilight I fear will often reappear,
O how can my soul lost be found at any cost?
The new cannot efface the old tear-shedding trace;
One broken heart yearns for the other kept apart.
When spring sets in,
Fragrant as is my skin,
My girdle turns loose for my waist grows thin.

Teng Bin

TUNE: UNIVERSAL JOY

Lotus blooms fade,
Green plane leaves fall
Hills on hills appear lean;
Woods on woods cast less shade.
Of what avail
Are the fame and gains small
Like the horn of a snail
Or the head of a fly green?
Why not get drunk with the poet in his east bower,
Among chrysanthemums in flower,
Why not till with plough in hand
A few acres of land
With your yellow buffalo?
Why don't you homeward go?

Deng Yubin

TUNE: CHATTERING SONG
(I) AT LEISURE

Deep in the mountain under the clouds white,
In thatched cot I fear nor summer nor winter night.
At leisure I talk with woodcutter and fishermen;
Drowsy, I sleep' neath trellis of gourds now and then.
Do you not know,
Do you not know?
It's better than to rest in anxiety and fright
On waves high and low.

TUNE: CHATTERING SONG
(II) O WORLD

Nothing but air
Is enveloped in your skin;
Your dry bones bear
Nothing but sin on sin.
For your children you may do right or wrong;
You'd shoulder mountains a fortune to win.
Do you understand my song,
Do you understand my song?
Do nothing silly if you want to live long!

Ali Xiying

TUNE: JOY BEFORE PALACE
MY NEST FOR IDLE CLOUD

In my Nest for Idle Cloud,
Sober, I drink and write; while drunk, I croon aloud.
I will not read nor on lute will I play,
Nor dream to climb up high.
I will make merry at leisure,
And let sun and moon like shuttles pass by.
Wealth and rank, after all,
Like flowers, will bloom and fall.
The prime of youth has passed away.
What should I do if not seek pleasure?

Feng Zizhen

Tune: Song of Parrot
(I) A Hermit's Pleasure in the Mountain Pavilion

I move my house atop the frowning hill;
As a woodman I am a green hand still.
I play chess till flowers fall from old trees,
Branch on branch, leaf on leaf, in rain and breeze.
My friends would call me back, but I say
I'd rather stay.
Pointing to clouds and hills before my door,
I need not pay for the scene I adore.

Tune: Song of Parrot
(II) Parting Grief

Your dappled horse neighs when I ask you to stay.
I fill your cup with wine to detain you in vain.
The green willows will see you go far, far away
To see the Sunny Pass dotted with morning rain.
I complain why, without turning the head, the wild geese
Should fly away one by one with the vernal breeze.
Gazing on the bridge, I wipe with my sleeves tear on tear.
Soon I find the Pavilion of Adieu is near.

Zhu Lianxiu

TUNE: SONG OF LONG-LIVED SUN
REPLY TO LU ZHI

O countless mountains

And wreaths of smoke!

Languid becomes the man in broidered cloak.

I lean on the casement like heart-broken fountains.

O could I be released with the waves going east!

Guan Yunshi

TUNE: AUTUMN SWAN ON FRONTIER
WRITTEN FOR A FRIEND

In the west breeze shiver a few dots of wild geese.

It breaks my heart to think of the Southern Dynasties.

I spread out paper fine to write down heart-felt line.

Without inspiration, I put down my pen.

When I was in the mood to write then,

I would wipe all stains away.

How can I be so sick at heart today

As to write only two words I would forget:

"Everlasting regret."

TUNE: EMBROIDERED RED SHOES

To you I cling, on you I lean,
We sit side by side by the window-screen.
I snuggle up to you and into your embrace,
We sing against the pillow face to face.
I listen, count, worry and fear night will soon pass.
Night passed, but love is not allayed, alas!
Love not allayed, time flies away.
O Heaven, why don't you lengthen night into day?

TUNE: FALLING MUME BLOSSOMS

When comes the autumn new,
We have just parted.
Along the endless river floats the moon broken-hearted.
The eastward-going painted ship has bid adieu.
This is only the first night I'm longing for you.

TUNE: SONG OF MOON PALACE
PARTING SPRING

I ask the Eastern God where's the end of the sky.

At sunset cuckoos cry,

On running water fall peach blooms,

Dim, dim distant hills loom,

Sweet grass seems filled with gloom,

Rainbow clouds thick with fumes.

Where is the willow down blown away by the breeze?

In whose house floats gossamer over the trees?

Tired of playing on the lute's string,

I lean

Against the swing.

The moon shines on my window screen.

TUNE: SONG OF CLEAR RIVER
THE MUME BLOSSOMS

The southern branches of mume trees

At night are the first to blow,

Revealing vernal beams.

They love the company of moon and snow,

But will not play with butterflies or bees.

Sometimes their gloomy fragrance steals into our dreams.

Zhang Yanghao

TUNE: TRIUMPHANT SONG
HAPPY RAIN ON THE FIRST DAY OF THE FOURTH MOON

All plants wither and dry,

Rain falls to wet the earth.

All revive' neath the sky;

The wind and cloud bring mirth.

The peasants dance

In wornout cloak of bamboo.

I'm happy in a trance,

Knowing not what to do.

TUNE: SONG OF DAFFODILS

I am retired when I've just passed mid-age;

As paradise I look on my hermitage.

How lovely hills and rills outdoors appear!

There's nothing to offend the eye and ear.

It is true joy to think over and understand:

A golden belt may gird you with distress;

Woe may be hidden in violet official dress.

Why not wear a ratten cap, cane in hand?

TUNE: SHEEP ON THE SLOPE
THINKING OF THE PAST ON MY WAY TO TONG PASS

Peaks like brows knit,

Angry waves spit.

With mountain and river far and near,

On the road to Tong Pass I appear.

Gazing on Western Capital,

I hesitate, alas!

To see the place where ancient warriors did pass.

The ancient palaces, hall on hall,

Are turned to dust, one and all.

Before my eyes,
The empire's rise
Is people's woe;
The empire's fall
Is also people's woe.

TUNE: SKYWARD SONG

Willowy shores,
Bamboo-lined stream,
The sun sieves green and golden shades as in a dream.
Cane in hand, slowly I go to the fishing place
To watch at leisure
Gulls and herons play with pleasure.
Peasants at the plough and fishermen on the oars
Do not know they are in a picture fine.
If with such a scenery you sit face to face,
You will get drunk without wine.

Bai Bi

Tune: Song of Parrot

Living at Parrot Islet as I can,
I am an illiterate fisherman.
My leaflike boat braves the perilous waves.
I've slept through Southern rain and smoke.
My eyes are filled with green mountains when awake;
I come back, shaking water off my green straw cloak.
In bygone days I blames Heaven by mistake.
See how well He disposes me!

Zheng Guangzu

Tune: Song of Moon Palace

(I)

My saddle laden with dust and outworn sable coat,
I wield my tired whip where reed catkins float.
Shivering with my sword and bow,
Straight into mist-veiled rainbow-clouds I go.
It moves a roamer's heart
To see the wheat undulate in the western breeze
And hear the reed rustle by the stream clear.
A thousand dots of cold crows on old trees,
Two or three rows of cawing wild geese
Fly through cold air and fall on the sand.

(II)

West of the winding shore near the whirlpool
Fishermen cast their net or fish with rod and line.
East of the dim bridge by the sand fine
A few bamboo-thatched cottages stand.
All over hills and vales full
Of red leaves and flowers in yellow dye.
In such a season sad and drear,
From home I'm far apart
At the end of the sky.

Zeng Rui

From Blaming My Gallant to Song of Picking Tea
Hearing the Cuckoo in My Boudoir

(I) Tune: Blaming My Gallant

How pitiless is naughty cuckoo's cry!
It has assailed my ears from on high.
Cry on cry has vexed me and broken my heart.
O cuckoo, how could you know the reason why
I feel a boundless grief to be kept apart!

(II) Tune: Gratitude to the Emperor

The curtain hanging low,
Tightly closed doubled door,
The winding balustrade
And the sculptured eaves fade.
West of the painted bower you sing,
Awakening me, drunk in spring,
From my morning dream.
Do you not know
I cannot stand, night and day, any more
Your vexations like a stream?

(III) TUNE: SONG OF PICKING TEA

O When have I
Left the embroidered screen?
Why should you cry
To me: "Better go home!"
My gallant in the south is entranced in love scene.
Why don't you cry to him not to roam?

PALACE GRIEF
(I) TUNE: MEETING OF GOOD FRIENDS

Gloomy, I mount the tower, lean on the balustrade
And view the evening scene:
The sky is wide, clouds blend with water green.
The shadow of the bower drowned in the pool,
The wild geese write slanting words on clouds white.
The withered willow trees caress windows and door;
The lotus fades before waterside pavilions cool.
The dreary scene adds to my grief without words.
Going down, I pace in courtyard steeped in moonlight.
My ringing pendants startle the birds,
The crane cries and echo the bells of jade.

(II) TUNE: JOY OF FREEDOM

Seeing the gloomy scene, I'm sad as phoenix green.

From heaven I'm kept far apart

As if imprisoned in the phoenix town.

Could I have a happy marriage with my mate?

I'm so much grieved that tears like rain stream down.

Drunk with brimming cups, when will wake my heart?

I hear the water clock of jade stop

Dripping in the western breeze drop by drop.

Midnight just passed away,

It is colder than autumn late.

O when will break the day?

(III) TUNE: FRAGRANCE OF GOLDEN CHRYSANTHEMUM

How can I stand

The autumn crickets' chirping shrill,

And crows in palace trees cawing still?

Going to lonely bed, how can I sleep?

My soul is seized by Lovesickness deep.

How can I go to the dreamland?

(IV) TUNE: A GOURD OF VINEGAR

I cannot fall asleep
Nor sit with ease till deep
In the night I remain
Heartily sick without physical pain.
My heart will not consent
To my stifling awhile my lovesick sentiment.

(V) TUNE: HIGH LEVEL EPILOGUE

The green flame of the flickering candlelight grieves
The incense burned up in the censer of gold.
In the courtyard run riot withered leaves,
The pale pillars caressed by bamboos tall.
Can it be true that woman can fight the gloom?
Can I resist dreariness, lean as I loom?
Laden with grief, I am heart-broken;
Drowsy and sick, when can I be awoken?
Though the wind is light in the painted hall,
My green quilt is still cold.
How can it warm up my stockings at all?

(VI) TUNE: EPILOGUE

Sleep will not come to me at all;

My maid will not answer my call.

Incense burned up, lights out, I feel chill, sad and drear.

Only the sympathetic Moon Goddess

Pities my loneliness.

She sheds through my window screen slanting moonlight clear.

Sui Jingchen

THE EMPEROR'S HOME-COMING

(I) TUNE: WHISTLING AROUND

The village chief announces from door to door:

Whatever errand no one should refuse to run.

The errand's not an ordinary one:

Rootless fodder be collected on the one hand;

On the other messengers should meet the demand.

Hard to deal with! they say.

The royal cortege will come

With the emperor to his home

Today.

The village elder holds an earthen plate,
The busy young man a gourd of wine.
They wear the hood washed of late
And stiffened silk shirt fine.
All play the rich though they are poor.

(II) TUNE: PLAYING THE CHILD

A blind man leads men and women in strange array,
Pellmell they beat the drum and on flute they play.
See a troop of horsemen
Arrive at the gate then,
And at their head
Many banners outspread:
On the moon flag a frosty hare in a ring white,
On the sun flag a golden crow in crimson light,
On the wind flag a cock dances and sings,
On the tiger flag there's a dog with two wings,
On the dragon flag you will find
A snake around a gourd wind.

(III) TUNE: LAST STANZA BUT FIVE

Fork painted red,
Axe silver-white,
Melonlike hammer and spearhead
With stirrup bright
And plume fan white like snow,
These flag-bearers forward go,
Holding unknown staffs in a mess
And wearing motley dress.

(IV) TUNE: LAST STANZA BUT FOUR

In the shafts steed on steed,
In harness there's no ass.
A crooked pole supports a yellow canopy.
Before the carriage eight officials lead;
Behind follow attendants in livery
And charming maid and lass
In the same dress,
With hair in tress.

(V) TUNE: LAST STANZA BUT THREE

From the carriage a big fellow comes down,

Saluted by all the people from the town.

That fellow seems not to see those who kowtow.

With legs apart the village elders deeply bow,

To help them up that fellow forward goes.

Suddenly I look up, who knows!

And gaze at him for long.

My breast nearly bursts with anger strong.

(VI) TUNE: LAST STANZA BUT TWO

"Your name is Liu,

Your wife is Lü.

I know the root of your family tree.

Fond of wine, you were chief around ten *li*.

Your father-in-law taught children to read.

You lived east of my farm to feed

Cattle for me and cut fodder for the cow

And till the land with the plow."

(VII) TUNE: LAST STANZA BUT ONE

In spring you gathered mulberry,
In winter you borrowed millet from me.
You bought on credit countless rice and wheat.
Renewing contract, you took more hemp by cheat;
Paying your debt, you stole more beans and peas.
Why should you play the fool, please?
It's registered in account book.
If you do not believe, just take a look!

(VIII) TUNE: THE EPILOGUE

You should at once pay the money you owed me,
And reduce the taxes on my millet and pea.
I only tell you, Liu the Third,
Holding you tight, I won't release you on your word.
Why should you change your name
And steal an emperor's fame?

Zhou Wenzhi

Tune: Chattering Song
Grief in Autumn

The iron bell on bell on the eave rings pellmell;
The crickets chirp so shrill chills my heart still.
Drizzling rain drips and drops but never stops;
Plane leaves fall in shower from hour to hour.
Alas! how could I fall asleep?
Alas! how could I fall asleep
Alone on lonely pillow when night is deep!

Tune: Song of Frontier

Turning up candlelight,
Standing by cloudy screen,
Heart-broken, I'm accompanied by shadow lean.
Awakened from thin wine,
For vain sweet dreams I pine.
Why should the slanting moon be bright?
I'm gloomy and depressed all through the night.
How lovesick I'm for you who won't come here!
The west wind blowing through the door brings me chill.
Iron bells ring across the curtain still.
O hear!
Is it the pendants of my dear?

Qiao Ji

TUNE: SONG OF CLEAR RIVER
(I) REFLECTION

I grow so lean for I think of you hard,
Though only by a wall we're barred.
I use as ink dewdrops which drip
From my pen-tip
To write a verse on the petal of flower
And ask the swallow to send it to your bower.

TUNE: SONG OF CLEAR RIVER
(II) VERNAL VIEW

Thousands of emerald branches of willows weep
For they're grieved not to keep
Late spring from going.
In tears they bid adieu to water flowing
With grief-laden fallen red
Last night's riverside shower shed.

TUNE: SHEEP ON THE SLOPE
THOUGHTS IN WINTER

(I)

You change along,

Take right for wrong,

Too foolish to know weal from woe.

With fortune made,

You love fair maid.

Gold only props you up to wanton time;

Wealth piled up only leads to crime.

Body in jail,

Heart will not wail.

(II)

For a month I've left home,

Lodge in hospice and roam.

Where can I get a frugal meal without pay?

Shunning society,

Without old company,

From whom can I borrow when I've spent my gold?

Again it's winter solstice today.

Where's wine on credit sold?

Where's mume against the cold?

(III)

In winter day
Snow melts away.
Who is accompanying mume blossoms lean?
I moor my boat
And fish afloat.
The frosty wind has pierced my straw cloak green,
When fish comes to my hook, O look!
My head bitten by breeze,
My hands, frost-wrinkled, freeze.

TUNE: SONG OF FLOWER SELLER
O WORLD

My hardened heart's like iron in the stove,
Wealth and rank like butterfly once dreamed of,
Glory and fame but shadows in wine-cup.
Sharp wind and snowflakes down and up,
Cold meal left o'er,
In dimly-lit bamboo-fenced cot I shut the door.

TUNE: LEANING ON BALUSTRADE
(I) YEARNING IN SPRING

Under pale moon by pear blossoms on rails I lean,
My silken stockings cold with clear dew on moss green.
Grief-stricken, I am in sad plight,
Still I burn incense for him at night.

TUNE: LEANING ON BALUSTRADE
(II) A YOUNG SONGSTRESS

With flowers over the head and clappers in hand,
Singing spring songs, of grief she does not understand.
From painted bower her song streaks the sky.
How could the morning orioles not feel shy?

TUNE: LEANING ON BALUSTRADE
(III) ON MY WAY TO JINLING

I roam on a lean horse laden with verse I write;

Tired birds bewail over desolate villages in sight.

Overhead willow down in flight

Adds to my forehead hair white.

TUNE: PLUCKING LAUREL BRANCH
(I) EVENING VIEW

A tired roamer on southern shore,

I climb up high.

How many heroes sank of yore!

How can I bear to buy

Arable land and field

And hang my sword on the tree not to wield?

Whose house is steeped in brilliant sunset glow?

Whose heart is loyal as the hook-like moon hanging low?

Lamplight deep hidden behind the window screen,

I only see the phosphorus light green,

And hear the scream of ghost unseen.

TUNE: PLUCKING LAUREL BRANCH
(II) ON CELEBRATION TOWER

Like fleecy cloud flying down from the southern sky,
Her shadow fair reveals she's shy.
Refraining from smile, she begins to sigh.
Orchid scent around her forehead,
Her dress fragrant with flowers overspread,
The soul of mume blossom disturbs her dream.
She looks like the goddess in love along the stream,
And meets her lover, herb in hand, in fairy land.
A wreath of gloom has left its trace,
The pillow hides her leftover grace.
Half drunk, in twilight she is sunk.

TUNE: PLUCKING LAUREL BRANCH
(III) ROAMING ON MOURNING DAY

Pear blossoms fade in wind and rain.

On narrow window frame I lean

By delicate window screen.

In what mood before lamplight can I remain?

A roamer whose head on the pillow lies,

And whose heart to the end of the earth flies.

My grief as long as an old man's hair white,

Fifty years have passed like a vernal dream overnight.

Suddenly a house comes to sight,

Where smokelike willow leaves

Adorn the tilting eaves.

TUNE: PLUCKING LAUREL BRANCH
(IV) THE RIVERSIDE LAND

I ask people by the riverside why

Mume trees are not

Planted near by.

The trunk of old mume tree is used to support the door,

Wild weeds are overgrown along the shore.

Dreary is the bamboo-fenced cot.

On the roof of the godless temple foxes trot;

Officials doing nothing let rats run in the hall.

Around the yellow sand white water flows.

Leaning on the balustrade, I count all

The crying crows.

TUNE: COURTYARD FULL OF FRAGRANCE
SONG OF A FISHERMAN
(I)

I bring fish to buy wine:

Fish delicious and fine,

Strong wine intoxicates.

I have no meat of whale in my plates

But sturgeon salted or just fried.

The waves of the lake make my wine cup shake;

The shadows of hills fall by my boatside.

Come back ashore,

I bring my rod with fishing line,

Careless of sorrow now and of yore.

(II)

Waves make my pillow quiver,

The moon wanes on the river,

I see far-off hills shiver.

None could forbid running water or floating cloud;

I'm better than the lord of woods or mountains proud.

The rainbow cloud steeped in cold waves look like brocades;

The autumn moon like molten gold on the sea fades.

Who will drink my home-brew

Together with me?

Who but the gull of the sea.

TUNE: JOY BEFORE PALACE
THE FIRST TOWER OF THE LAND

I beat on rails,

The foggy wind blows on my hair and the sea wails.

I croon aloud, dispersing startled cloud.

Counting the mountains blue,

I point to fairy isles coming in view.

Wearing my silk hood high,

I'm used on the crane's back to fly.

Raising my head, I utter a long sigh,

And straight ascend the sky.

TUNE: RED PEACH BLOSSOMS
IN TIP-TO-TOE STYLE

Petals fall with willow down outside the screen,

The screen is still and on closed door I lean,

Leaning beside the mirror, I feel shy,

Shy to see my beautiful face, I sigh.

Sighing, I count when my lord will be,

Will be back to see me.

O me who wonder only,

Only how he can leave me lonely.

TUNE: SONG OF DAFFODILS
(I) SEEKING FOR MUME BLOSSOMS

From village to village through hoar winter I go;
North and south of the stream my shoes are white with snow.
Where but in Lonely Hill can I find her fair from tip to toe?
Her fragrance comes when I feel the cold wind blow.
Suddenly I meet her in silk robe and white sleeves.
Sober from wine, I wake from dreams, but then she leaves.
My heart is broken to hear the flute wail
In twilight when the moon turns pale.

TUNE: SONG OF DAFFODILS
(II) WRITTEN FOR A FRIEND

Illness and parting grief disturb your tender heart.
When can you meet again now you are kept apart?
You may open a lovesick shop in southern town,
And go to seek amusement when grief weighs you down.
But grief like goods is stored up on your eyebrow.
How can you pay the tax on the tea? How
Can you slide the weight on the steel yard?
To change account books is really hard.

TUNE: FROM FALLING SWAN TO TRIUMPHANT SONG
FAREWELL RECALLED
(I) TUNE: FALLING SWAN

Thank you for your verse on leaf red
In cold place where yellow blooms spread.
Clear stream and sky are paper white,
On which wild geese and clouds would write.

(II) TUNE: TRIUMPHANT SONG

Where have you gone since our adieu?
Where can I send you my verse new?
Sober from wine when lamplight gleams,
By window cold I wake from dreams.
I pass
In mind what happened these ten years.
Alas!
On my forehead grey hair appears.

TUNE: MEETING OF GOOD FRIENDS
PARTING UNDER WILLOWS RECALLED

(I)

East of the bridge we do not like the willows green.
How many parting lovers they have seen!
Willow down wafts like snow on sunny day,
My heart gone with it far, far away.
The willow twigs, though long, cannot retain
His parting steed; green clouds veil the bower in vain.
I roll up my sleeves and pluck with my hands fair
A tender sprig swaying in the east wind, where
I see two hearts into a knot are tied
And an embroidered ball hangs by the side.

(II) TUNE: JOY OF FREEDOM

Now I cannot tie a lovebirds' knot,
But startle a pair of birds in love
On the tip of the tree above.
How can my grief be forgot?
I listen to golden orioles sing,
They remind me of the sweet songs of spring.
But I'm afraid they would break
Your dream and wake
Your parting grief on the green leaf.

(III) TUNE: A GOURD OF VINEGAR

My tears are dried after the rain,

My frowning eyebrows shy remain,

Loving and complaining of the flowing breeze.

Ill in autumn, how can I feel at ease?

Before autumn comes, how languid I look!

Like the waning moon hanging on the hook.

(IV) EPILOGUE: COMING WITH WAVES

I don't want you to lean on fragrant balustrade,

Or stand on mossy, stony path in the green shade.

I want you to gaze afar and wait all day long,

To remember our farewell feast and farewell song.

As for today,

I want you to tie your boat in the green shade,

When you return from far away.

Liu Shizhong

Tune: Joy Before Palace

With face drunk red,

In village elder's house tax-collectors come and go.

Some officials sit in the hall,

With heavy bags of tiger skin piled up below.

They call the roll, but none answers at all.

They shout and cry

Until their throats go dry.

Then soldiers would damage the crop and horses tread

The field so that nothing could grow.

Aluwei

Tune: Falling Mume Blossoms

A thousand years after,

All will pass in laughter.

Only burnt paper money would waft in the breeze.

Though cuckoos cry out blood among the mist-veiled trees,

How could they retain

A vernal dream vain?

Wang Yuanding

Tune: Drunk in Time of Peace
Cold Food Day

Nursling crows caw out cry on cry,

Breaking the early day of spring.

Last night the drizzle moistened the sand far and nigh,

Thousands of homes sweetened by the breeze on the wing.

The lovebirds tiles of painted house are washed clean,

The colored ropes of the swing wet before the bower.

I wake to find the sun redden the window screen

And hear the street cry of selling apricot flower.

Xue Angfu

Tune: Autumn Swan on Frontier

Busy for far-flung fame as swallows in flight,

Culture hangs by a thread, none cares to be polite.

Time flies away as fast as flashing light,

Like frosted silk the hair on our forehead turns white.

All say it is good to retire,

But to be a hermit none has the desire.

Up to now only

The poet-hermit still feels lonely.

TUNE: FROM FAR-FLUNG SOUTHERN SKY TO SONG OF CLEAR RIVER
FAREWELL TO SPRING
(I) TUNE: FAR-FLUNG SOUTHERN SKY

I have a mind to say farewell to spring,

But I have no means to stay her lingering.

Spring will come back again next year,

Would it not be better to stay forever here?

Peach blossoms seem to know my grief,

Falling like red jade petal on petal, leaf on leaf.

I gaze as far as the Southern sky,

But I can't see the way spring will go by.

(II) TUNE: SONG OF CLEAR RIVER

If spring had a heart, she would feel sadder still

To see time fly away,

The sun go down from hill to hill,

And water flow from rill to rill.

But where, where is the place for her to stay?

Wu Hongdao

TUNE: GOLDEN CANON

(I)

Fallen petals fly away with the breeze,
But leaves are still fresh on the trees.
The waning moon will wax again,
Wax and wane,
But we can't gather round as the moon waxes round.
Rosy faces to grow old are bound,
But where could youth be refound?

(II)

No more village brew?
Undistilled wine will do.
The wood I cut sold out,
Heigh!
I'll have money in my pocket, no doubt.
If you want to drink, you need not pay,
But take your gourd and follow my way.

TUNE: UNBROKEN STRING
LEISURE AND PLEASURE

(I)

I pass my life
On floating raft
Steered by the autumn breeze on the River with pleasure.
Despite the smoke, my young son is brewing tea aft,
Cooking fish in moonlight, busy is my wife.
Drunk, we talk at leisure.

(II)

Careless of gain and fame,
To rank I lay no claim.
Poet Tao would not in official work be lost,
Nor let bookworms eat holes in his books,
Nor his chrysanthemums be bitten by frost,
He returned to his nooks.

Zhao Shanqing

Tune: Plucking Laurel Branch
Hall of Lake and Hill

Outside eight windows water dissolves in moonlight,

Orioles and swallows dance on the stage in a line

Before poets and drinkers of wine.

The dancers' fans bring a breeze light,

They dance like clouds or pear blossoms white,

With fragrance sweet their powdered faces spread.

The old state replaced by the new with candles red,

The white-haired still remember its newly built hall.

Dancers in their changed palace attire

Awaken envious flowers' desire,

But lakes and hills care not for the state's rise and fall.

TUNE: INTOXICATED IN EAST WIND
AN AUTUMN DAY ON MY WAY TO XIANGYIN

In face I see green hills piled up on hills green,

Nearby grass grows waist-deep and grassy isles are seen.

Frost-proof tangerines and shaddocks stand proud,

Reeds steeped in rain look clear and clean.

Across the waves the riverside tower dimmed by cloud,

Peeping through boundless autumn on the river, it grieves

To see a few withered willow leaves.

TUNE: BLESSED EASTERN PLAIN
MOORED BY THE POST

The beetles still,

The crickets trill,

Clear autumn shut outdoors in night tranquil.

Where is the Phoenix Tower high?

Grieved to see parapet nigh,

I dream to be a butterfly.

My homesickness for ten long years

In tonight's alien dream appears.

Ma Qianzhai

Tune: Song of Willowy Camp
Written in Time of Peace

By Phoenix Tower's side,

With frontiers pacified,

What with the world in peace can I do after all?

My office resigned,

Leaving the capital,

I'm glad again a rural life to find.

Too proud to imitate the poet planting flowers,

I will grow melon outside the east door.

With fruit-bearing trees before my bowers,

And mulberries at the foot of the hill,

I will pass still

The rest of my years as of yore.

Zhang Kejiu

Tune: Man and Moon
(1) Written in the Mountain

The rise and fall from year to year are but vain dreams.

A poet's eyes are tired of roaming on the streams.

The sage's forest grows old,

The ancient palace overrun with weed,

The temple crows feel cold.

A few rooms in a cot are what I need;

With my ten thousand books,

I'll retire in my nooks.

What can I do in the mountain?

With leaves of pine

I'll brew my wine,

And make my tea with vernal water from the fountain.

TUNE: MAN AND MOON
(II) RHYMING WITH A FRIEND IN LATE SPRING

Lush, lush sweet grass and spring clouds spread pellmell;

Grief seems exhaled by setting sunlight.

In the pavilion where we drank farewell,

I see no painted boat on the calm lake afloat,

Nor the proud steed neighing beneath willow trees.

I only hear the cry of birds in fright,

The dripping rain leftover last night,

And the sigh of the eastern breeze.

All the peach flowers are blown away.

Where is the beauty of the bygone day?

Within the closed door only the fallen reds stay.

TUNE: MAN AND MOON
(III) A SPRING DAY ON THE LAKE

From my bower girt with mountains green,

The far-off Southern sky cannot be seen.

My love as fair as jade white

Came into my dream last night.

Where is she now playing on the flute far away?

Before the door night and day,

I see but heartless autumn moon

And faithful vernal tide at noon.

How languid now am I!

My heart like flowers that can't fly,

My eyebrows like willow leaves dry.

TUNE: DRUNK IN TIME OF PEACE
(I) THINKING OF THE PAST

A floating boat,

A gull carefree,

I climb the height with endless sorrow old and new,

White clouds linger with me.

From Phoenix Tower I find the changeless hills blue;

Beside the swing within the wall

The weeping willow slender grows;

Before the pavilion late autumn flowers fall,

But heedless, the endless river still flows.

TUNE: DRUNK IN TIME OF PEACE
(II) REFLECTION

Poverty is disliked by all.

Is money not dear to you?

If a crystal ring in a pot of paste should fall,

Could it not be pasted in view?

If a writer advertises for a millionaire,

His soul is puzzled with money and renown.

A sleepy head cannot be fair and square,

It would be safer to hold a gourd upside down.

TUNE: ORANGE AND MUME ON BROCADE

Her perfumed pink cheeks look like rosy cloud,

Her ebony chignon like black crows in crowd.

I guess

She must be a songstress

In such a picturesque attire.

Her emerald headdress quivers with each pace,

Her dainty silken robe is large and light.

How bewitching is she walking in delight!

How could I not steal glances at her face?

How could I quench my insatiable desire?

TUNE: GREETING A FAIRY GUEST
AUTUMN NIGHT

After rain it turns fine,

All steeped in bright moonshine.

The fragrant autumn courtyard hears the beetles pound.

Deeper, deeper the night,

Deeper, deeper the sound.

It breaks the heart of those who part,

But cares not for their plight.

TUNE: EMBROIDERED RED SHOES
(I) AT THE FEAST OF MARSHAL NING

I longed to ring my pendants in the Gallery.
Now old, the forest under white cloud pleases me.
Who of the youth still knows the ancient heroes' deeds?
Their precious swords like blue serpents fade,
Broken to pieces are their robes of brocade,
The flying dragons now become stabled steeds.

TUNE: EMBROIDERED RED SHOES
(II) ON MY WAY TO THE TIGER HILL

Where may I moor my boat along the ancient shore?
Where is my friend in the blue mountains I adore?
Can I draw pictures in poetic lines?
At the song of wild geese the reed grows old,
At the sight of herons the knotweed feels cold,
At dusk the cranes return to their nest amid the pines.

TUNE: PLANE LEAVES
(I) LAKE AND HILLS AT NIGHT

After dusk apes sing,

Men seem to go along a screen,

No temple bells ring.

Peaks on peaks like bars in wet green,

Pines echo with the breeze,

Cold jade plays on lonely plane trees.

I seem to be in the Moon Palace Hall

Turning fragrant in the fall.

TUNE: PLANE LEAVES
(II) THINKING OF THE LUTIST

Where is my lutist bright?

Grass grows again in spring,

But dust covers the lute's string,

The parting grief embodied in willow leaves,

She wipes her tears away with lotus sleeves.

My soul can only croon in the mume bower white,

The cloud-veiled Southern mountains lost to sight.

TUNE: PLUCKING LAUREL BRANCH
(I) FAREWELL AT THE WEST FERRY

Our parting grief outweighs your painted boat.
I'm still at Ferry West,
Your sorrow eastward flows.
On my steed I won't ride,
Nor open tearful eyes.
I fear to lean on rails of tower high.
Spring comes and goes,
The willow trees by riverside
Are grieved to say goodbye.
The tide may fall and rise,
The heartless gulls still float.
The mist-veiled water runs without rest.
I can write verse for you,
But how could we not say adieu?

TUNE: PLUCKING LAUREL BRANCH
(II) THE MOUNTAIN-CLIMBING DAY

Before blue hills I put down my official hat;

Returning wild geese fly across the autumn sky.

How can a tired roamer not think of his own flat?

Though the rainbow-colored sleeves try

To fill my golden cup with wine,

And jade-like hands play on lute fine,

I'm growing old, my white hair wafts when west wind blows.

Tomorrow yellow blooms will sadden butterflies.

Looking back to the far-flung skies,

I find the setting sun in bloody dye,

Dotted with a few chilly crows.

TUNE: PLUCKING LAUREL BRANCH
(III) RHYMING WITH A FRIEND

I'd call the Beauty to go to the west with me.

How can I not delay on the winding long way

Along the careless mist-veiled stream, carefree,

The cuckoos cry amid green trees,

The blue sky streaked by wild geese,

The gulls are friendly with snow white.

Drunk, I lean on pear trees in blossoms bright,

But willow trigs cannot tie the boat with moonlight.

I try to go upstairs to gaze far, far away,

But find the Southern Rivershore with green overspread

And vernal grief fading in fallen red.

TUNE: PLUCKING LAUREL BRANCH
(IV) RURAL LIFE

Wicker gate closed, I'm proud to croon' neath rainbow cloud.

Forest and peaks dimly appear,

With fairy cottages far and near.

White clouds beyond my bower overspread,

Before my window green bamboos stand,

In the tripod is left cinnabar red.

None of my household grows melon in the waste land,

In my cot I drink tea with my friends day by day.

Spring has nearly passed away.

After the blooming rose, now all

The pear blossoms will fall.

TUNE: SONG OF DAFFODILS
DRINKING BY MUME TREES

Good flowers will open in the rain;
Good friends from afar come again.
In rhyming with your verse I owe you a year-old debt.
Let us drink our fill now we've met.
The balustrade winds round the bower of carved jade,
Over young trees butterflies flit about.
The ground dotted with green moss looks like deer skin.
Let us tread on it till our shoes are worn out.

TUNE: RED PEACH BLOSSOMS
PARTING GRIEF

The autumn rains have oldened yellow flowers,
Careless of those in lonely bowers.
My tears stream down to hear the song played by sad strings,
Putting down the lute and turning on lamplight, I feel shy
To see the picture on the screen
And hear the bell of jade rings.
My grief has wetted the silk handkerchief green.
Why could I not go with you to the end of the sky?

TUNE: UNIVERSAL JOY
(I) THE WEST LAKE

The pearly palace hall

In fairy island looms.

In the shade of the green pines tall

Wafts the fragrance of pink lotusblooms.

Cloud on cloud woven in brocade

Like frozen Silver River in the boundless sky,

Two beauties in flowing robes on phoenix wings fly,

And play on violet flute a tune to chill the moon.

The evening breeze caresses the balustrade,

Lotus girls' songs waft low and high,

Fishermen's lanterns float east and west, far and nigh.

TUNE: UNIVERSAL JOY
(II) AUTUMN THOUGHTS

Love poems show anew
The debt I owe you.
On flowery paper with ivory pen I write,
With golden hairpin and jewel case in sight.
Wild geese cry past the full moon bright,
But you are beyond the mountains blue.
What with my parting grief can I do?
Up the tower I go.
The west wind cannot blow my grief away.
Will the white-gowned messenger come today?
I have at least the hedge in the east
Where yellow chrysanthemums will blow.

TUNE: WELCOME TO SPRING
(I) AT AN INN IN JINHUA

A fine rain brings down red flowers on mossy way,
And the west wind blows willow down away.
How sad and drear to pass a lonely Mourning Day!
How could I bear to hear all the night long
The cuckoos' home-going song!

TUNE: WELCOME TO SPRING
(II) AT AN INN IN YONGKANG

Rain beats on lotus leaves drop on drop
Like thousands of pearls without stop.
The mountain's clad in cloud like a cloak of jade.
I try hard to write a verse to describe the scene.
On the slope with grass green,
I hear beyond the pines songs of tea-picking maid.

TUNE: SKYWARD SONG
A WIFE WAITING ON HER LORD

Of whom will you pencil the brow?
I know with whom you are in love now.
Deep in the lane I hear your horse neigh,
Drunk at midnight, you're on your homeward way.
I take great care to make your bed,
But you pretend to turn away your haughty head.
Who is so unashamed as you? Unworthy, you know it's true
I've done my best,
So by lamplight you lie down, not yet undressed.

TUNE: SHEEP ON THE SLOPE
A WIFE BORED

Her chignon loose as cloud,
Her lovebirds quilt with fragrance overflowed,
Her boudoir closed, she's deep in vernal sleep.
Willow down flies,
Her young maid cries:
"Lo! What auspicious snow!"

It wakes her from the dream of her love she will keep.

"Who?

What a bore!

Oh,

It is you."

TUNE: JOY BEFORE PALACE
LONGING

The sandbar veiled in moonbeams,

I confide to my lute my tears of ten long years.

Lovesick, I will not gaze on the picturesque screen.

For far away, my love cannot be seen.

Spring wanes with cardamom flower;

I send him a lovebirds handkerchief from my bower.

Now fragrance of rapsberry is cold.

Where are the scenic spots of old?

I find but window-screened morning dreams.

TUNE: SONG OF CLEAR RIVER
HOMESICKNESS IN AUTUMN

From far-off home a letter comes in western breeze,
Asking me when I can be home-bound.
In the sky reddened by maple leaves cry wild geese,
Drunk amid yellow flowers strewn on the ground,
I hear in autumn dream rain beat banana trees.

TUNE: SUNNY SAND
CALLING ON A HERMIT

Green moss and old trees in deep gloom,
Pale clouds and far-off water loom,
Red leaves cast shade on little room.
Who'd cross the creek but those who seek
The mume in bloom.

TUNE: LEANING ON BALUSTRADE
A NIGHT ON THE STREAM

The moon shines bright on water clear,
Who's playing the lute on the stream?
It moves to tears those who hear;
Their sighs mingle with each moonbeam.

TUNE: A SPRIG OF FLOWERS
RETURN FROM THE LAKE A

(I)

Rainbow clouds fall from endless sky;
Autumn's mirrored in far-flung stream.
Her rosy face looks like flower in dream,
Her flossy hair like far-off mountains green
Or colored screen.
Roadside pines in cold emerald dye,
Black brow overshadows smiling eye.
Coming with my love fair and tender,
Need I envy mume blossoms sweet and slender?

(II) TUNE: SONG OF FRONTIER

I linger amid flowers, holding her hand fair,
And drink in silver cup, sitting in cozy chair.
The Moon Goddess, leaving her lord, lonely appears.
I think of the young beauty without a peer.
Where is she now passing her declining years?
The brilliant talent at the height
Of his renown admired the Lady of the West
Whether richly adorned or plainly drest.

I come here with my love at leisure,

We write verses by fountain side with pleasure.

On the fifteenth night before flowers and moon bright,

Her fingers playing on fourteen strings bring a breeze light.

How lovely they seem!

Her ivory clappers accompany her song of frontier.

The night tranquil,

All mountains still,

We hear the fountain sob with running stream,

The monkey cry

And the crane sigh.

(III) TUNE: EPILOGUE

The golden bell in rocky temple rings,

The crystal palace quivers on the lake.

Night air fresh turned,

From wine I wake.

The incense burned,

Water clock sings.

When we come back in laughter, it seems midnight or after.

Is it not better than to go

To seek mume flowers on the bridge cold with snow?

Xu Zaisi

TUNE: UNIVERSAL JOY
THE MOON OVER THE RAINBOW BRIDGE

Cold is the moon,

Pot frozen soon.

Jade hare amid the cloud,

On water dragon proud.

A pot of wine,

Three lute songs fine

Wake up the fairy queen from her sweet dream

To tread on the waves of the stream.

I lean on rails, my face by divine breeze caressed,

Bower and tower far and nigh,

Earth and sky low and high,

And rivers east and west.

TUNE: WELCOME TO SPRING
MOORING AT NIGHTFALL

Water in east and west creeks are shallow or deep;

Clouds over mountains far and near come and go free.

A boat passes the fishing beach in autumn breeze.

I peep

At dusk through mist-veiled trees,

And find two thatched huts or three.

TUNE: SONG OF MOON PALACE
(I) TEMPLE OF A LITERARY GENIUS

You wrote with brilliant pen on ups and downs.

It won your age-old vain renowns.

Come back from your dream,

Why at your loss should you be sad,

And at your gain be glad?

What is the use of your gloom?

Beyond the setting sun the hills appear green still,

Beside the bridge the temple ruins loom.

Your words flow like pearls in a stream;
Drunk, you spilt your ink at will.
Is it not better to be a man of men,
Who for the sword gave up the pen?

TUNE: SONG OF MOON PALACE
(II) LOVESICKNESS

In early life I knew not what lovesicknes is.
When I began to know a bit,
I fell heart and soul into a fit.
My body like cloud white,
My heart like willow down in flight,
Floating as gossemar light.
In vain a wreath of fragrance is left here.
When will my noble roamer reappear?
When comes my disease,
Can I know what time it is?
It comes by dim lamplight,
When the moon is half bright.

TUNE: SONG OF DAFFODILS
(I) RAINY NIGHT

I hear autumn's sigh in a plane's shivering leaf;

I see raindrops on banana as drops of grief.

After midnight I dream of home-coming at midnight,

Chequers are left on chessboard by candlelight.

How can a chequered man in an inn not sigh?

Ten years like a dream on the pillow pass by.

Old parents far apart

Now come into my heart.

TUNE: SONG OF DAFFODILS
(II) LOVE IN SPRING

I am as lovesick as I'm full of care;

We long for each other here as there.

Ten years of courting give me as much joy as pain;

Our life is chequered with loss as well as gain.

There is not half a thing which brings me not half shame,

In autumn late I regret autumn flame;

In springtime fine I complain I'm sick of spring wine.

All my life long is nothing but a love song.

TUNE: MAN AND MOON
THE ANCIENT TEMPLE OF SWEET DEW

By riverside stands ancient Temple of Sweet Dew,

Invaded by autumn hue.

Ruined walls overgrown with wild grass,

Empty gallery paved with fallen leaves, alas!

Oldened steps covered with moss green.

No more tourists are seen.

Down in the west the sun goes,

The river to the east flows.

Only the magnolia blows.

I ask the monk for whom

The flowers are in bloom.

TUNE: SKYWARD SONG
WEST LAKE

In inner lake

And outer lake,

There's nowhere but spring is awake.

True hills and water make the picture true,

No carved jade can outdo.

It's good for verse and for wine,

Rain or shine.

It is a place where gold may be spent,

And brocade used as ornament.

Oh! poet Su,

Mume-lover Bu,

You might still find your willows' gloom

And flowers' tomb.

Zha Deqing

Tune: Half and Half
Spring Attire

She tries to compare herself with the willow tree,
And holds a twig to see which reveals vernal glee.
Finding herself less lovely than crab-apple flower,
Again she makes up in her bower,
Powders her face and rouges her lips with grace.

Tune: Song of Willowy Camp
The Ancient Capital at Jinling

Coming to ancient capital,
I find nothing but ruined wall,
Grieved that Six Dynasties have passed like running stream.
Things have changed and stars turned around;
Men live not so long as towns stand.
History is nothing less than a game of chess.
Soon we wake up from our vain dream
To find on northern land but burial mound,
Which mountains on four sides surround.
How many trees grow
High and low?
Who is grieved over the waste land?

Tang Yifu

TUNE: A SPRIG OF FLOWERS
(I) COMPLAINT AGAINST SNOW

Is snow of any good?
No bumper year's foretold.
It brings the poor no food
But makes the hungry cold
As of old.
Aimless, it falls along the street;
Carefree, it flies to any place.
It knocks on window-panes with unseen feet,
And steals indoors without leaving trace.

(II) TUNE: SONG OF FRONTIER

You cling to thatched cot,
And pierce into leaky wall,
Frivolous as wave on wave of willow down.
Have you ever been close to noble son's gown
Or quilt of brocade light,
Or kept company with fishermen old
In straw cloak and hat of bamboo?

You do what you will with the wind roaring loud

In company with heavy cloud.

You care not for the poet frozen on his ass,

Not knowing what to do;

Nor the mume-lover Lin Bu

Shivering with cold;

Nor the banished scholar barred on his way

At the Blue Pass.

Long lasts the night;

Late breaks the day.

My poor quilt is not,

Not warmed at all.

How can I fall asleep

Even when night is deep?

Your skin is cold and hard as iron or stone,

How dare I cling to you alone?

(III) TUNE: EPILOGUE

All winter long I am in heavy debt for wine.

I can't go home for you've barred my way for miles and miles.

You fruitless flower, can you last for years?

Though you may wander from day to day,

At last I will sweep you away

And heap you up into piles.

Cold as you are, when the day is fine,

I'll warm you up and dissolve you into tears.

Zhu Tingyu

TUNE: SUNNY SAND
AUTUMN

In the courtyard the leafless plane trees loom;

By waterside all lotuses are in full bloom.

The frost-bitten maple leaf knows my heart,

Willing from its bough to part

And fly down for me to write verses on.

Zhang Mingshan

Tune: Universal Joy
(I) Apart in the World

O peony flowers!

O moonlit bowers!

Bright flowers can be bought when they are desired;

Bright moon cannot be brought down when admired.

You may see full-blown flowers from the balustrade,

And drink to the full moon when you gather round,

The moon may wax and wane, flowers may bloom or fade.

What gnaws our heart is to be torn apart.

Faded flowers may blow again when spring comes around;

The waning moon may wax full on Mid-Autumn Day.

O When will you come back now you are far away?

TUNE: UNIVERSAL JOY
(II) GRIEF AT HEART

Wind roars;

Rain pours.

Wind tears my dream apart;

Rain breaks my tender heart.

Wind soughs in gales among plane trees;

Rain falls drop on drop on banana leaves.

Wind accompanied with rain grieves;

Rain saddens, rolled up by dreary breeze.

How can I bear wind and rain?

Whatever I do, they remain.

I'd bear them now and again.

TUNE: UNIVERSAL JOY
(III) TO A FUNNY TUTOR

You teach pupils to read and write,

And they learn to recite,

To obey their fathers and mothers,

To be good towards their brothers,

To serve their prince to the end,

And not to find fault with their friend.

Well bred, you make a pose all the day long,

Lest people should say you are wrong.

You tell the pupils: "Your work should be well done."

But they say: "The work is a tedious one."

And the father says, "All is up to my son."

Yang Chaoying

TUNE: SONG OF DAFFODILS
MUME BLOSSOMS AT WEST LAKE

The sky and earth look like icy pot after snow.
To seek after mume blossoms in West Lake I go.
Treading on snow by the brook on an ass I ride,
I've outdone the poet's picture of the lakeside.
I bring a pot of wine where mume blossoms throng;
Wine cup in hand, I smile at the flowers for long.
Wine drunk up, l may pawn my sword to buy;
Drunk down, by lakeside I would lie.

Song Fanghu

Tune: Sheep on the Slope
A Carefree Dream

Blue hills greet and love me,
With white clouds above me.
I do not dream of golden belt or violet dress,
But of a thatched room,
With wild flowers in bloom,
Careless alike of rise and fall, of failure and success.
In simple food and plain living I'll find delight.
Of poverty I would make light;
Success can't raise me to the height.

TUNE: SONG OF CLEAR RIVER
TO THE MOON

So round is the full moon in the sky.

I bow and whisper to her in view:

"You must be forever round on high,

And never wane to the eye!

I wish that those in love shall gather round as you."

TUNE: FIGHT OF QUAILS
PARTING

(I)

At sunset stretch out disant hills

And far-flung mist-veiled rills,

But few temple bells ring

With drumbeats watch-towers bring.

A leaflike boat

Rows away and afloat.

How drear and sad

Our parting song!

Our short meeting so glad,

Our separation so long!

(II) TUNE: VIOLET FLOWERS

My slender, slender body wastes away;
The chilly, chilly nights longer stay.
In lonely, lonely bed warmth is worn out.
Will the moon and flowers feel shy at my sight,
And wild geese and fish take flight?
I doubt.
From now on who will send a letter to me?
I fade without glee.
The blue bridge is drowned in the stream
When I awake from my sweet dream.

(III) TUNE: SONG OF FLIRTATION

How to give relief
To my heart-felt grief?
The farewell song with three refrains heard,
My thousand threads of sorrow stirred,
I'm grieved to see countless evening clouds above,
They remind me of where we were happy in love.
Where will you moor your boat in the moonlight?
Are you missing me by the reedy shore tonight?

(IV) TUNE: THE BALD HEAD

I dare not raise the eye

To places of delight.

Looking back, I find gloomy our rendez-vous.

With whom could I talk in moonlight and starlight?

What can I do

But give sigh on sigh?

(V) TUNE: SOVEREIGN OF MEDECINE

Do not make haste!

The bitterest grief makes my jade-like body waste,

My illness more severe,

My head less clear,

And gnaws my heart till my pearl-like tears fall.

So idle and so drear,

I would not mount my fragrant cab at all.

(VI) TUNE: EPILOGUE

How can I bear with open eyes to see us part?
To leave my flute companion would break my heart.
Hardly have I not heard the wind to say goodbye,
When grievious rain makes half the river run high.

Jia Gu

TUNE: FROM DRINKING SONG TO EMBROIDERED RED SHOES
FOR GOLDEN ORIOLE

(I) TUNE: DRINKING SONG

Like flatfish or twin branches of a tree,
We were as happy as a pair of swallows free.
My parting boat left you alone on shore, alas!
Gazing as far as west of the Sunny Pass.
Our love like Yellow River keeps on flowing;
The Middle Mountain can't bar it from growing.

(II) Tune: Embroidered Red Shoes

Remember when night was deep,

All fell asleep,

You came alone.

Come, you spoke but two words or three;

Gone, you got a verse from me,

It would be kept at heart till we are dead and gone.

Zhou Deqing

Tune: Autumn Swan on Frontier
By the River of Xunyang

For miles and miles the endless river flows silk-white;

Dots on dots of southern hills stand indigo-blue.

Sails on sails go past as fast arrow do;

The waterfall dashes down like lightning from the height.

All evening clouds turn into dew;

The crescent moon imitates a bow;

The wild geese from the frontier fly in a row.

TUNE: COURTYARD FULL OF FRAGRANCE
ON THE TOMB OF GENERAL YUE

By word and sword he tried

To rebuild the royal temple's fame,

And left in history an undying name.

But envied by traitors before he had won,

He was treacherously slain,

Leaving unrecovered the lost Central Plain,

And Northern royal tombs not visited again.

His work undone,

The dreary wind and drizzling rain

Are weeping for the General buried by lake side.

TUNE: PLUCKING LAUREL BRANCH

Leaning on windowsill, speechless I sigh.
Without the seven necessities,
How could households be called families?
The fuel is as dear as wood cut from on high,
Oil as nectar of dew,
And rice as pearls all new.
The sauce is used up in the jar,
The salt bottle is empty, you see,
There's no more tea,
Nor vinegar.
I can hardly afford these seven necessities,
How could I enjoy flowers and willow trees?

Ban Weizhi

Tune: A Sprig of Flowers
The Zither Heard on an Autumn Night

(I)

On window screen the breeze sways shadows of willow trees;
In wide sky the moon round casts plane's shade on the ground.
On chiseled plate of gold incense is burned and cold;
The bronze dragon sobs when icy waterclock throbs.
From where comes the zither song?
It's echoed loud and clear among the clouds for long.
It wafts with the light breeze far and near.
The divine music has just reached my ear,
My body seems to float in celestial sphere.

(II) TUNE: SONG OF FRONTIER

It's like cold fountain splashing on the stone,

Phoenix and pheasant singing in the moon,

Or pearls rolling in plate of gold.

It stops the steed running in wind so cold,

Startles the fish swimming in the pond

And wild geese flying on horizon and beyond,

And detains the cloud floating atop the trees.

It's word on word is clearly heard.

How can we bear its heart-rending tune?

It's drear as the Princess' lament on the frontier,

Clear as the prince playing on his jade flute,

Melodious as the lover's moonlit lute.

Listen again and you will be startled anew,

It is the song of Sunny Pass bidding adieu.

You will be grieved to hear the lovers say goodbye,

All hidden in your heart would burst into a sigh.

All dust washed away, what care have you?

(III) TUNE: EPILOGUE

Her fair fingers lightly touch the icy strings;
I'd write to her a letter interwoven with flowers,
Remembering the young writer in his bowers.
Who can be this lover of springs?
O why so lovely should she be!
Her song sinks me into and wakens me
From my dream of butterfly on the wings.

Wang Yuanheng

TUNE: DRUNK IN TIME OF PEACE
Disgust with the World

I hate flies striving to suck blood,
And black ants fighting for food.
A brave man will retire at the high tide,
And not follow the old rut or drift along,
I sigh for mansions to lords no longer belong,
And fear blue hills into hostile states divide.
I dislike dragons mingling with snakes in the dust.
As an old man, I'll leave them with disgust.

TUNE: SKYWARD SONG
HERMITAGE

Glory is but a dream,

Rank and fame paper torn,

Right or wrong mountain-high tide.

Why should my horse have trod frosty royal streets down?

How many times have I heard cocks crow at dawn?

All cloaks and crowns will be outworn.

Why not retire on the lake or the stream?

Why fall into the royal snare of renown?

I'd like to be hermit by the hillside.

Pitying heroes slain in palace sad.

I'd rather resign or pretend to be mad.

TUNE: INTOXICATED IN EAST WIND
RETURN TO MY FIELD

I'd live far from the crowded market town,

and near green hills and blue rills up and down.

Cultivated into a wild man with hair grey,

I'd get rid of modern official way,

And learn to sing a shepherd's or woodman's song.

Drunk all day long,

Beside my earthenwares,

I would not fall into the mundane snares.

Ni Zan

TUNE: MAN AND MOON

Startled on my pillow from my dream
Of bygone years by fishing song at southern stream,
I see peak on peak veiled in clouds like a screen,
And pool on pool seem overgrown with grass green.
How much it grieves
My heart to think of my house of yore
Overshadowed by plane leaves.
With doors hidden amid willow trees.
At ease,
I am oldened in vain.
What can I do but listen to the rain
Or see flickering lights on river shore?

TUNE: RED PEACH BLOSSOMS

On autumn stream pale smoke and cold mist rise,
With water crystal-clear and silk-white.
A few rows of wild geese bring parting grief to the eyes.
After snow the sunny sky's bright,
Green duckweed and red knotweed high and low appear.
The rower sings a Southern song on the stream,
So plaintive and so drear,
A white gull's startled from its dream.

TUNE: LEANING ON BALUSTRADE
FOR A FRIEND

My friend is good at playing on the flute green,
It may bring down the moon on misty stream in spring.
Why can it not attract the fairy queen?
In cloud and water you may hear jade pendants ring.

TUNE: SONG OF DAFFODILS

The east wind can't bring flower to her small red bower;
The mountains bar the sky like eyebrows in green dye.
The cold spring cares not of the slender blooming tree,
The heartless water flows away, carefree.
A pair of tender swallows whisper on the beam,
Awaking her from her sweet dream,
Where can she find her lover? Look!
The setting sun seems to hang on the curtain's hook.

Liu Tingxin

Tune: Plucking Laurel Branch
Parting Recalled

Parting's the greatest grief in life, alas!
Don't sing thrice the refrain
Of farewell song of Sunny Pass!
Worried to death, I wipe away my tears;
At a loss, I stroke my chin and ears;
Stupified, I shut my mouth tongue-tied.
My love for you, you should keep in heart;
Of ill and pain I would bear my part.
Of household work, you need not care a grain.
But don't forget to bring me word now and again!
If I know you are in love with another flower,
At once in cab and horse I'll leave my bower.

TUNE: SONG OF DAFFODILS
LOVESICKNESS

Oh, deep regret

On regret deep

I can't forget!

At dusk it overwhelms my bower and I weep.

Piled-up sorrow,

Sorrow piled-up,

Sorrow lasts till the morrow,

It drinks my blood in emerald cup.

I am idle,

Idle am I,

Made up, I would sidle;

Incense burned, I would sigh.

I shed tears,

Tears are shed,

My face appears

Tearful as if with water overspread.

I am ill,
Ill am I,
Languid still,
My heart would utter cry on cry.
I see the bloom,
The bloom sees me,
Languid and lean she'd also be.
I and the moon,
The moon and I,
Looking in my face, she'd feel shy.
I ask the sky soon, It won't reply,
For like me it's also in deep gloom.

TUNE: A SPRIG OF FLOWERS
FAREWELL TO SPRING

Thread by thread willow twigs sway in the breeze,

Drop on drop falls the rain on pear trees.

Pear petals fall with the rain,

The wind goes down with willow down.

Springtime has passed in vain.

What can I do when it has passed?

Why has it gone so fast?

I ask the Eastern Lord in power,

Who cares for wailing bird and weeping flower?

Tang Shi

TUNE: MINOR FRONTIER
CROSSING THE RIVER ON MOUNTAIN-CLIMBING DAY
(I)

I sail a lonely boat on the stream in autumn breeze,

The misty water runs without cease.

Heart-broken, I have no verse to write on tower high.

Lean mountains seem to sigh,

Like me are grieved old trees.

When drunk before my cup, I smell at dogwood spray,

Asking how many friends have their heads turned grey,

I may seek pleasure again,

But friends are not the same as then.

When yellow flowers bloom once more,

Who would enjoy with me their beauty as of yore?

(II)

In autumn breeze my lonely boat sails on the stream,

Boundless the mist and water seem.

White clouds westward go

While wild geese southward fly,

I open the window, lo!

The waves with my thoughts surge up high.

Like poet Tao I'd drink before flowers in bloom,

Wasting my time on Mountain-climbing Day.

So sad and drear,

How can I not waste away?

The chrysanthemums are also in gloom,

In vain they smell sweet as last year.

TUNE: SONG OF CELESTIAL FRAGRANCE
RIVERSIDE TOWN RECALLED

How I adore the capital on rivershore!

It was an earthly paradise,

With eastern head and southern end so nice.

Thousands of homes with painted beam and pearly screen,

Hundreds of winding bridges over water green,

Embroidered dragon boats for miles and miles overspread.

Along the swaying willow trees,

Among the blooming flowers red,

The violet steeds were running in the vernal breeze.

With ringing pendants of jade

And pearls and earrings bright,

The fragrant sedans vied in beauty with moonlight.

No more dance and songs in light or shade,

None could retain good times of yore.

Magnificence has gone with the declining day;

Splendor like running water has passed away.

Lan Chufang

TUNE: FOUR PIECES OF JADE
A MAID IN LOVE

(I)

His love is true,
His heart good too.
I only want him to make it clear,
If our love's known, I fear;
Gossip makes me feel shy,
Questions make me sigh.
If he's not seen, I blame he's late;
When we have met, I hesitate.
Is it true I won't satisfy him till I die?

(II)

Stupid in all am I,
Ugly all in all is he.
Our love is true though stupid and ugly are we.
He wins my love despite his ugliness;
He loves me for my stupidity none the less.
Such a pair of ugly man and stupid wife
Cannot be found in earthly life
But in the paradise on high.

Zhong Sicheng

Tune: Intoxicated in Time of Peace
A Beggar-Scholar

(I)

I go along the street,
Enter a house and drag my feet.
I ask if there's a charitable miss
Who'd give me a hearty meal overdue,
Embroider a love-knot of bliss,
Make a coverlet new,
And go be bed hand in hand with me?
Oh! help the poor, my dear grannie!

(II)

The poor may be happy in love,
The rich are stupid high above.
I would repair an old brick-kiln with clay,
And open a school for beggars by day,
I'll put on a black hat half outworn,
And a yellow cloak half torn
With a disjointed belt ill at ease.
I'd teach the beggars to enjoy the moon and breeze.

Qian Lin

TUNE: WHISTLING AROUND
THE MISER

(I)

Can you tell truth from lies, the foolish from the wise?

The miser stinks of gold since days of old.

He is greedy for wealth at the expense of health

As if he hated to have money circulated.

He never feels shame

To thrust his hand to snatch money out of the flame,

Or from a sea of blood upsurging high.

How could he lag behind indeed?

He contrives intrigues day and night,

And seizes money by hook

Or by crook,

And seeks profit as tiny as the head of a fly,

Or a grain of dust raised by the hoof of a steed.

Insatiable to pile up wealth to his last breath,

Careless alike of life and death,

At last he brings but shame to light.

(II) TUNE: PLAYING THE CHILD

God helps those who, content, won't complain of poverty;
Piled-up riches invite regret and woe.
A sage with his counters of ivory
Calculated without rest night and day,
Careless if time with sun and moon will turn away.
He'd toil with all his force for his sons like a horse.
Thin he would grow,
Careless alike of his clothing and food,
Only over money would he brood.

(III) TUNE: LAST STANZA BUT NINE

The vernal hue on his cheeks fades away;
Autumn frost is sprinkled on his hair by and by.
His gloomy eyebrows frown all the day;
He would lend at fifty per cent interest high.
He wished the goods in pawn unredeemed a year long.
As cruel as a wolf strong,
He would press oil from people's bones
In spite of their loud groans.

(IV) TUNE: LAST STANZA BUT EIGHT

He has a mind to be a baron high,
But he is called as "rich as half a state."
Why should he bear hunger and cold
To pile up a mountain of gold?
And hire guardsmen ringing bells at the gate
For fear his money-dragon away might fly?
He would invite Taoist priests to use magic art
To keep it from flying apart.
He snashes his teeth, walking to and fro,
Planning to have all income and no outgo.

(V) TUNE: LAST STANZA BUT SEVEN

He feels no shame to do what is to blame,
And injures his health for ill gotten wealth.
He does not care for others,
Even his uncles, aunties, sisters, brothers.
He would outshine the richest man in Golden Valley fine,
But not care for the poor scholar ill at an inn.
He has no friend or kin,
He only loves the beauty with bright eyes and teeth white,
But shares with none his fur coat and carriage light.

(VI) TUNE: LAST STANZA BUT SIX

"The more profit you obtain,

The more you still want to gain.

You'd carry on a strife at the risk of your life.

Though you have field on field, you are not satisfied;

On your shelf there are books on which you won't take looks.

You pretend to enjoy chrysanthemums by fenceside,

But you're a pseudo-bard,

A disguised leopard."

(VII) TUNE: LAST STANZA BUT FIVE

"You wish to turn the endless river into wine,

To pile up gold as date-palms you incline.

You're cursed by others for the money they owe you;

For a loan of millet you lose kins old and new.

For a bundle of hemp you turn friend into foe.

What woe!

You're blindly arrogant and greedy.

In the end you'll become careworn and needy."

(VIII) TUNE: LAST STANZA BUT FOUR

"Fortune amassed made Han Premier burned up when dead,

And Tang Minister lose his head.

Piled-up wealth, if not distributed, would bring woe,

Though gold and jade are heaped up high from town to town,

Soon wild grass and weeds there will be overgrown.

However rich you may grow,

You will be annoyed

For the wealth unenjoyed."

(IX) TUNE: LAST STANZA BUT THREE

"One day good or ill fortune will fall by fate,

You are bound to die early or late.

Wealth will be spent faster than made.

Do not forget what's said

Of the beauty jumping down from tower of jade

Before she sang in golden tent a new song.

Do not forget what's wrong:

On the one hand women plunged into the well,

On the other men were battered pellmell."

(X) TUNE: LAST STANZA BUT TWO

Through broken windows all away would fly,
And chairs and tables moved out in a gust,
Gold, silver, money, rice would turn to dust.
Monsters from forests and mountains would cry;
Orphan would follow Widow Star in Milky Way.
Noisy all day,
Spirits of flowers would bewitch the hosts;
Storehouses would be stolen by wasteful ghosts.

(XI) TUNE: LAST STANZA BUT ONE

Disasters fall from angry skies;
Guilty and put in jail, he tries
To bribe with money, but to no avail.
Nailed on the wooden ass,
In vain he begs to drive lightly the nail,
And to hang him up softly by the hook.
He can by no means be forgiven, look!
His wandering soul flies,
And then dispersed, alas!

(XII) TUNE: LAST STANZA

His wealth amassed all his life is put on display
To testify his guilt.
His corpse is-exposed without a quilt
In public place by day,
Sunburned and wind-bitten till its decay.

Sun Zhouqing

TUNE: SONG OF THE MOON PALACE
DELIGHT IN THE MOUNTAIN

In my round thatched cot in face of the col nice,
I cook my rice
With bamboo of the mountain,
And brew my tea with water of the fountain.
I eat potatoes sweet, onions, chives and fruit,
And enjoy mountain flowers in view,
I listen to ice crack under the moon new;
Clouds swept away by mountain breeze
Startle crows from the trees.

The mountain hue so green,

Can I not feel proud

Of the mountain scene?

Beyond the mountains spreads the sunlit cloud;

There're cottages at the mountain's foot.

Cao De

TUNE: BLESSED EASTERN PLAIN
THE RIVERSHORE

Among the thatched cottages low

There is a shop selling wine.

When comes a drinker, they will soon uproll

The curtain red.

In endless sky the rainbow clouds overspread,

Ducks sleep here and there around a pond square,

Over old trees hovers crow on crow.

It's like a poetic line

Or a painter's scroll.

Zhen Shi

Tune: Thrice Drunk and Sobered

I was a bright pearl in my parents' palm.

How could I sink low in mansions of dreams?

It is my duty to please men by my beauty,

But behind them my tears fall in streams.

Homeless for three long springs, far from the southern land,

How, driven by the east wind, could I stand?

I'm further grieved

To find no one to pay a lot of pearls as alm

That I may be relieved.

Wu Xiyi

Tune: Sunny Sand
Written at Leisure

On thousand-mile-long River pass east-going sails.

How many times at Sunny Pass has blown west breeze?

Still I see a world of dust to my disgust.

At sunset cry the newcome wild geese.

What can I do but beat now and then on the rails.

TUNE: SONG OF THE CLEAR RIVER
AN AUTUMN NIGHT

White wild geese fly pell-mell like autumn snow;
In the cool night clear dew-drops grow.
Drunk, I tread on the pine-tree's root steeped in moonlight
And wipe the stone clean of cloud white.
Under the starry sky sleepy I lie.

TUNE: SONG OF LONG-LIVED SUN
FOUR SEASONS (AUTUMN)

Grief heavy on my heart
Can't be written in word.
What can I do to keep autumn apart?
Beyond my painted bower is heard
The newcome wild geese's cry.
They bring no letter but write "loneliness" in the sky.

Cheng Jingchu

Tune: Drunk in Time of Peace

The endless grief weighs on her heart in palace deep;

In silence she dreams of royal cab drawn by sheep.

Before the lonely Gate grows green grass sad and drear;

The setting sun lingers, only spring wind comes here.

Her streams of tears have specked the jadelike bamboo;

Gloomy, she goes outdoors, having nothing to do.

She takes a stroll at leisure,

And gazes on the smoky scene without pleasure.

Oh! what she sees

Is drizzling rain and evening breeze

And petals falling from pear trees.

Anonymous

TUNE: SONG OF DAFFODILS

(I)

Green hills are veiled in mist along the far-flung stream,
On Mountain-climbing Day I stand in foreign land.
A lonely man in lonely boat by lonely town,
However hard, can my heart not break down?
Two streams of tears have blurred out autumn light.
The golden dream,
Is sweet but for one night.
This Mountain-climbing Day is passed just as the last.

(II)

The sun sinks in the west while the stream eastward flows.
Nothing achieved, on my two temples white hair grows.
Heart broken, I am thinner than a yellow flower,
Fearful of the coming of Mountain-climbing Day,
Forced to climb up high, my thoughts go back to my bower
In my native land thousands of miles away,
I would lean on rails of twelve towers in autumn breeze,
Why should I be grieved and feel ill at ease?

(III)

I often remember our feast of adieu
When we mingled our tears with wine new.
I would break all green willow twigs before we part,
To write down as my pen what's on my heart,
Can I find paper as big as the sky above?
Could it contain my endless regret and love?
I can only write down two words: "Love birds."
In vain I croon the love of the breeze for the moon.
On whom can I depend my love letter to send?

TUNE: PLUCKING LAUREL BRANCH

(I)

How many in the world are people unwise?

Most of them early rise;

Few are idle guys.

Some bewitched by women and wine lose their health;

Others are greedy for wealth.

The living to death are bound;

The dead are sent to burial mound.

Carriages and horses welcome the new,

The crafty will deceive you,

The uncrafty will forgive.

If you do not know how to live,

You are a swam living in vain.

(II) SLIGHT SNOW

The northern wind blows snow down like silver sand,

It erodes the steps where I stand,

Passes through the screen, caresses willow trees,

And startles crows. It's light as feather of geese,

As willow down it's tender,

And as pear flower it's slender.

Heaven pities the poor and sheds only snow slight,

To announce a bumper year to the farmers' delight.

A few jade petals in full bloom

Adorn the branches of a tree.

It would be easier for the poet to seek mume;

It's not enough for a scholar to brew his tea.

TUNE: AUTUMN SWAN ON FRONTIER
(I) ON MY WAY IN THE MOUNTAIN

On eastern way, on western way, on southern way,

Five miles away, eight miles away, ten miles away.

I go slow-paced, I stop slow-paced, I look slow-paced.

Suddenly the sky is effaced,

The sun effaced, the clouds effaced,

The earth is paved with departing sunbeams;

Turning my head, I find mist grow as dreams.

Does mist not veil the countless hills and rills?

Does it not veil my heart which untold sorrow fills?

(II)

My love for him is like moonrise,

My joy like brows above the eyes.

Thinking of him, The Moon on West River I croon;

Waiting for him, my heart is like the waning moon.

Then he was highly pleased with me.

Now forsaken by him can I be?

Our reunion is like the moon deep in the sea.

TUNE: PLANE LEAVES
(I) SATIRE ON LIARS

In eastern village phoenixes are born of cocks;
In southern farm a horse changes into an ox.
In summer we wear furs lest we should freeze;
The roof is a good place to plant trees.
In a dry moat we may sail a boat;
In a jar we may bake bread and cook meat.
My eggplant is as big as melon sweet.

TUNE: PLANE LEAVES
(II) TO A GREEDY MAN

You weave a thousand plots one night,
And plan for a hundred years bright.
Your pit of hell is as deep as the sea.
On precious jade you pillow your head,
On a field of gold your feet tread.
One day when death befalls you, see!
What could stand you in good stead?

TUNE: CHANGES OF TUNES
(I) LOVESICKNESS

With eyebrows like two willow leaves
I frown, but I can't drown my lovesickness that grieves.
Since he went away,
Absent-minded, I do embroidery all day.
If Heaven knew the state of mind I'm in,
It would also grow thin.

(II) A TRYST

"Among flowers by the eastern wall in moonlight,
Remember such a lovely scene and lovely night!"
She whispers in his ear:
"Come earlier tomorrow, hear!
If you love me in doubt,
You will pass away as the light goes out."

TUNE: EMBROIDERED RED SHOES

(I)

One enjoyed wealth all men adore;
Another had no food in store.
Is Heaven just or unfair?
At thirty-two one lived in a house bare;
Another became premier at twenty-four.
Now both are buried in the open air.

(II)

Cutting down my lover's name,
I'm grieved to gaze at it again and again.
I burn to ashes these two words in candle flame,
And use them to powder my temples twain,
Or to pencil my eyebrows so that "you
Will never be out of my view."

(III)

You have heard one gossip or two;

For three days or four you came not to my door.

For five or six you thought the gossip true.

For seven times I bought tortoise shell to divine.

When I see you after eight days or nine,

I'm languid. Do you know how much for you I pine!

(IV) FOR A SONGSTRESS

The Long River can't carry my longing away;

The Middle Mountain can't bar our love in midway.

Deep, deep I think of you

In deep night of adieu.

Silence reigns far and nigh.

When you came by,

You said two words or three,

When you left me,

You left but a verse free.

I'll bear it in mind till I die.

TUNE: CELEBRATION OF IMPERIAL REIGN

I tell the old unsuccessful candidate:

Do not study too late!

One classic read, white hair grows on your head.

Why should you wait for three years for another exam?

Learn from what I am!

Do not participate!

TUNE: INTOXICATED IN EAST WIND
(I)

Songstress' throat tender

And dancer's waist slender

Are ready for flowers in the light of the moon.

I regret spring has passed too soon.

Let it not to swallows and orioles be known

That two-thirds of spring have gone away.

It's better to be drunk before flowers by day.

(II)

I'd wear my patched coat when the sun is high;
Your official hat is not cold-proof at midnight.
I'd till my field with my buffalo under the sky,
You might ride your steed neighing in moonlight.
I would toil hard and envy none who shine;
You might on blood-stained ground put up a fight.
I would lie drunk by the side of my jar of wine.

TUNE: SONG OF FRONTIER

Rich, you are called dear brothers;
Penniless, you're despised by others.
Good fortune's left to worthless son
Showing off clever things he's done,
It has proved of little avail
To kick the shuttlecock or play with quail.
He would not earn a living in his pawn shop,
But spend his money hard and soft without stop.
He has visited brothels from door to door
Till destitute, he is driven out by the whore.

TUNE: ASCENDING THE ATTIC
THE CUCKOO

I do not like to hear pitiless cuckoo cry,

Its home-going song breaks my heart.

It cries till no flowers bloom,

Till grief comes with gloom,

Till spring from earth will part.

"Why don't you tell my love at the end of the sky,

To come home lest I should die?"

TUNE: PARASITE GRASS

I would impart

To you what's in my heart.

Before God I cut down a wreath of my hair black.

Behind my parents we tryst at the foot of the hill,

Lonely and still,

With dew my stockings are wet.

Hardly have we met when we disagree.

If you regret,

Give back

My fragrant handkerchief to me!

FROM HAPPY THREE TO CHANGES OF TUNES

(I) TUNE: HAPPY THREE

Oh, lovely times and charming scenes change by and by;

Alas! the delights to the heart will pass away.

Man is fated to live, grow old, fall ill and die.

So let us make the most of each hour and each day!

(II) TUNE: SKYWARD SONG

O call a friend

And go on our way to West Lake today!

Let us drink up the pot of jade to the end!

Fragrant mist spread,

Petals fall red.

Even if you can live to ninety years,

The world still like an inn appears.

Count the three spring graces like dreams:

One-third passes with flowing streams;

Two-thirds with the dust.

Without our knowledge spring will pass in a gust.

(III) TUNE: CHANGE OF TUNES

In the west garden, cane in hand,
With endless grief I gaze into the far-off land.
Dancers are gone with fragrant willow down;
Songstress tired in her white silk gown.
Under crabapple flowers partridges cry;
Over willow tops cuckoos fly.
All call spring back and say "Goodbye!"

TUNE: READING GOLDEN CLASSICS

With fishing rod I earn a living without rest,
Coming and going east and west.
Wearing a straw cloak, I don't sigh
For I am poor. Old and drunk, I
Lie down in the breeze under willow trees.
On rippling waves afloat,
At dusk athwart the stream lies my boat.

TUNE: UNIVERSAL JOY

He is born with a fair, fine face,

Handsome in all, clever in word.

Lovely when he is heard,

Fickle in all he says.

Wherever he goes or stays,

Drinks or eats, I like his manner,

And follow him as a shadow under a banner.

I consider it as a favor

To absorb his flavor,

When he is honest, I appreciate his grace.

FROM FALLING SWAN TO TRIUMPHANT SONG
(I) TUNE: FALLING SWAN

From year to year we have grown old,

And day after day time is sold.

One autumn comes when another goes;

One generation after another grows.

(II) TUNE: TRIUMPHANT SONG

We meet and part

With joy or broken heart.

With a bed to lie on,

Our life is but a dream bygone,

Find a group of companions:

Now he or she,

Now you and me.

For friends we all shall be.

Now let's blow short or long,

Now let us sing a song.

TUNE: CHATTERING SONG
(I)

Yellow dust raised on royal road since olden days,

The graveside ruins steeped in departing sunrays.

A leaf falls on Black River with the western breeze,

The setting sun sheds light for miles on dreaming trees.

How can we not grow old,

How can we not grow old?

All hearts are broken for the heroes bold.

(II)

I cross the stream and follow the creekside pathway,
And reach the door where runs water jade-clear.
The green hills screen it from the world of dust red;
It can't be found for the ground's with clouds overspread.
I tell you it can't be found, my dear;
It can't be found, my dear.
In my cottage on Parrot Isle with none I'd stay.

(III)

Though I don't think of you, you appear in my heart;
When I think of you, can I keep langour apart?
How can my fragrant silk handkerchief stay
My tears streaming down from my eyes?
When can we beam with smiles and realize
Our love-birds' dream?
How can I not wish for such a happy day?
How can I not wish for such a happy day!
We who were happy by the side of lovely stream.

TUNE: THE FOUR GATES VISITED

(I)

The fallen reds on the ground look like a rouged face.

It's the best time to visit vernal place.

You fool don't know the rose has thorn,

But try to pluck crabapple flowers down.

See! my silk gown

Is suddenly torn.

(II)

In moonlight steeped crabapple flowers,

I have a tryst between the secret bowers.

Impatiently I wait for the one I adore,

Reading again the billet when comes Rose

To close

The corner door.

TUNE: THRICE IN JADE PAVILION

Bells hanging on the eaves ring in the breeze;

Rain beats loud on the green window without cease.

How can I bear alone the quilt and pillow cold!

How can I not blame the ungrateful gallant bold!

I can't keep him apart

With his divided heart.

Should he come to my place,

I would scold him without giving him grace,

Scratch him on the face.

And pinch his ears tight.

I'd ask him, "With whom did you pass the night?"

TUNE: SKYWARD SONG
REFLECTIONS

Those who can't read are powerful,

Those who can't write pass wealthy days,

The ignorant may win high praise.

Is it not Heaven's care to be just and fair?

How can He not know the good from the fool?

Why are heroes often frustrated

And talents not utilized?

The better they're, the worse they're fated.

What is the use to solve dispute,

Or have a virtue mute?

If you but do your duty, you will be despised.

TUNE: EMBROIDERED RED SHOES

Outside the window rain drips drop on drop;

Upon the pillow tears mingle with sigh on sigh.

Rain and tears hasten to fall without stop.

Rain makes the day more drear;

Tears with sighs seem to vie.

The window's not so wet as pillow with tear on tear.

TUNE: WELCOME TO SPRING
LONGING

I cut tight coat and skirt for fear I should grow thin;

I lightly pencil my brows to hide my chagrin.

O When I long for you, I mount the tower high,

Stand long and gaze far and nigh,

But I see only wild geese crossing autumn sky.

From Happy Three to Changes of Tunes
Parting Grief
(I) Tune: Happy Three

Since he left me, my brows are often knit.
When spring is gone, I close my red door.
The day is long in courtyard still, how can I bear it
For dusk is the time to deplore.

(II) Tune: Skyward Song

New traces and old
Of countless tears and grief untold,
How can I in lovebirds bed fall asleep?
You're printed on my lips and in my heart deep.
Alone I mount the tower high,
None cares for me.
I see the new moon atop the blooming tree.
With broken heart I gaze afar,
But I can't find where you are.
Oh, are you farther away than the sky?

(III) TUNE: CHANGES OF TUNES

The endless sky is

Barred with evening clouds and rows of wild geese.

We part more often than we meet;

My grief is longer than joy sweet.

I tell wild geese again and again, "If you see

My man, will you please

Tell him to write a word to me?"

FROM BLAMING MY GALLANT TO SONG OF PICKING TEA

(I) TUNE: BLAMING MY GALLANT

Of the four seasons only spring

Is dear and priceless;

The days are bright when sun and moon shine.

Maidens under willows look like a picture fine;

Some in brocade and others in silk dress,

All gather around the swing.

(II) TUNE: GRATITUDE TO THE EMPEROR

They talk in cheerful voice,

And make a lively noise.

Among them there's a palace maiden fair

Wearing a silk dress soft and red.

She grasps with grace the rope of colored thread,

And slightly pushes forward the swing,

Which goes as on the wing.

Her body slowly rises in the air.

Behold!

Her apron gauze still in her hold.

(III) TUNE: SONG OF PICKING TEA

All maidens vie

In swinging high.

Like rainbow clouds near to the sun they fly,

With body light and spirit bright,

Their grace would make the blooming trees feel shy.

许译中国经典诗文集

元曲三百首

许渊冲 译

五洲传播出版社　中华书局

序

"一个国家人民文化水平的高低,要看它对人类文化的贡献,也就是说,它对世界文化提供了多少珍品。"(引自1982年11月17日《人民日报》)唐诗、宋词、元曲就是我国对人类文化提供的珍品。

诗言志。孔子说过:"诗可以兴,可以观,可以群,可以怨。"这就是说,"言志"包括见物起兴,观察反映,合群交流,发泄怨愤。而在唐诗、宋词、元曲中,我们都可以看到"兴观群怨"的丰富内容。如以唐诗而论,李白的浪漫主义诗篇中有人与自然的交流,杜甫的现实主义诗篇中有对战乱时代的反映,白居易通俗易懂的诗篇中有对世风的批评,李商隐的象征主义诗篇中有心灵的感叹。如以宋词而论,则有缠绵悱恻的柳永,以理化情的苏轼,语浅情深的李清照,愤世嫉俗的辛弃疾。一方面,唐诗和宋词都继承了《诗经》中"兴观群怨"的文学传统;另一方面,又对元代散曲产生了重大的影响。

唐宋两朝是中国历史上的黄金时代,六百年间经济繁荣,文化发达,是全世界首屈一指的。而当时的西方正处在黑暗的中世纪时期。到了元代,蒙古族从北南下,侵入中原,统治全国,君临天下,压迫南方人民。现实社会中,蒙古人甚至可以随意杀死南人而不受惩罚,知识分子却沦落到了非常低贱的地位,甚至在妓女之下,只在乞丐之上。这种现象在元散曲中都有反映。如钟嗣成在《醉太平》中描写乞丐:

绕前街后街,
进大院深宅。

>　　怕有那慈悲好善小裙钗,
>　　请乞儿一顿饱斋。

又描写穷书生:

>　　风流贫最好,
>　　村沙富难交。
>　　拾灰泥补砌了旧砖窑,
>　　开一个教乞儿市学。
>　　裹一顶半新不旧乌纱帽,
>　　穿一领半长不短黄麻罩。
>　　系一条半联不断皂环绦,
>　　做一个穷风月训导。

又如真氏写一个妓女说:

>　　对人前乔做作娇模样,
>　　背地里泪千行。

由此可以看出唐代诗人的现实主义,到了元代,已经扩大深入到下层人民了。

　　元代知识分子一般无力积极反抗,只能愤愤不平地发发牢骚,以怨天尤人的方式发泄内心不平。如无名氏的《朝天子》中说:

>　　不读书有权,
>　　不识字有钱,
>　　不晓事倒有人夸荐。
>　　老天只恁忒心偏,
>　　贤和愚无分辨。

发牢骚后,他们尽量麻醉自己,把乐天知命、知足不辱当作处世的原则;把人生无常、消极的出世思想渗入自己的作品,主观幻想地美化田园的隐居生活。如冯子振在《鹦鹉曲》中写道:

>　　嵯峨峰顶移家住……

> 指门前万叠云山,
> 是不费青蚨买处。

他们做伴的是渔樵,流连的是诗酒,享受的是自然风光、田园乐趣,追求的生活境界是任情适意,逍遥自在。如乔吉在《满庭芳》中说:

> 白云流水无人禁,
> 胜似山林。
> 钓晚霞寒波濯锦,
> 看秋潮夜海熔金。

但是在自然风光中,他们并不能逃避现实,还是会遇到惊涛骇浪,废墟荒冢,使他们回到现实中来。如张养浩在《山坡羊》中写道:

> 峰峦如聚,
> 波涛如怒……
> 宫阙万间都做了土。
> 兴,百姓苦;
> 亡,百姓苦。

在自然中得不到安慰,有的诗人只好发思古之幽情,借古人的酒杯,浇胸中的块垒。如周德清在《看岳王传》中说:

> 功成却被权臣妒,
> 正落奸谋……
> 钱塘路,
> 愁风怨雨,
> 常是洒西湖。

在元曲中,我们可以看到唐代的英雄主义已经转化为悲观思想,宋代的理性主义已经转变成消极无为,他们抒发的情感大众化了,但他们的批评精神依然存在,他们的语体文风却又有新的发展。

以内容而论，元曲主要的题材是叹世和归隐；以形式而论，唱词多半用的是老百姓的日常口语。宋代的李清照早已用口语入词，如著名的《如梦令》：

"知否知否：

应是绿肥红瘦？"

但李清照的口语还比较高雅，我们再读张可久的《闺思》，那的确是用语极浅而意思极真了：

掩春闺一觉伤春睡，

柳花飞，

小琼姬，

一声雪下"呈祥瑞"，

团圆梦儿生唤起。

"谁？不做美？

呸，却是你！"

元曲和唐诗宋词不同的地方，是诗词韵分平仄，不能错押，有时可以转韵；曲则没有入声，平上去三声通押，一韵到底。而且用韵的密度较大，有时甚至是每句一韵。诗词尽量避免字句的重复，尤其是不能重韵；而曲却往往以重韵见长。元曲和诗词最大的不同，是曲在正规的格调之外，还可以加上一些衬字，使作者有更大发挥的自由。这说明元曲比诗词更加解放，更加先进，可以说是诗词的发展。这只要比较同一首曲子却有两种字数不等的曲调，就可以看出。如徐再思的《水仙子》：

九分恩爱九分忧，

两处相思两处愁，

十年迤逗十年受，

几遍成几遍休。

半点事半点惭羞，

三秋恨三秋感旧，

> 三春怨三春病酒,
> 一世害一世风流。

这首曲子只有八行五十五个字,而刘庭信的《水仙子》却有二十九行一百个字,由此可见刘曲比徐曲多了二十一行,四十五个字,如前四行:

> 恨重叠,
> 重叠恨,
> 恨绵绵,
> 恨满晚妆楼。

这几行就是把"重叠恨满晚妆楼"一行七个字扩大成为四行十四个字,增加的字和原来一行的字数相等,由此可见元曲衬字特点之一斑。

唐宋的律诗都以对仗见长,如杜甫"古今七律第一"的《登高》中最著名的一联:

> 无边落木萧萧下,
> 不尽长江滚滚来。

到了元代,对仗的种类也增加了,如"鼎足对",就是诗词中所没有的。它以三句为一组,互为对仗,往往形成对事物淋漓尽致的刻画,这又是诗词的发展。如马致远《夜行船》煞尾中的三句:

> 看密匝匝蚁排兵,
> 乱纷纷蜂酿蜜,
> 急攘攘蝇争血。

元曲可分散曲和杂剧两大类,散曲又可分小令、带过曲、套曲三类。小令只有一支曲子,带过曲是由两三支小令组成的,如《雁儿落过得胜令》由《雁儿落》和《得胜令》两支小令组成,《骂玉郎过感皇恩采茶歌》由《骂玉郎》《感皇恩》和《采茶歌》三支小令组成,所以可算是短套曲。套曲一般由四支以上小令组成,如杜仁杰的《耍孩儿》套曲由七支曲子组成，主题是《庄家不识构阑》，写乡下人进城看戏，颇像白居易现实主义的乐府。关汉卿的《一枝花》套曲却只包括四支曲子，主题《不伏老》，颇像嬉笑怒骂的辛词。马致远的《夜行船》包括七支曲子，主题《秋思》有苏东坡《赤壁怀古》的意味。曾瑞的《集贤宾》由六支曲子组成，主题颇有缠绵悱恻的柳词风味。睢景臣的《哨遍》包括八支曲子，主题是《高祖还乡》，在君道森严的封建时代，作者能够不从歌功颂德的角度来写汉高祖刘邦"威加海内兮归故乡"的盛况，而从一个过去与他有瓜葛的乡下人眼中，写出他装腔作势的可笑模样，显得非常新奇。乔吉的《集贤宾•咏柳忆别》，张可久的《一枝花•湖上归》，宋方壶的《斗鹌鹑》套曲都显示了元曲的抒情主流。钱霖的《哨遍》最长，包括十二支曲子，主题《看钱奴》是讽刺为富不仁的守财奴的。从本书选译的三百首小令和套曲，可以看出元曲和唐诗宋词之间继承和发展的关系。元曲发展的最高阶段是杂剧，最著名的代表作是王实甫的《西厢记》，国外评价很高，说是可和莎士比亚比美，却比莎士比亚早了两三百年，由此即可见中国文化之宏大发达。而元曲则和唐诗宋词一样，都是世界文化的珍品。

　　总而言之，元曲继承和发展了唐诗和宋词已有的"兴观群怨"的优秀传统：在意美方面，使诗歌更大众化；在音美方面，使韵律更自由化；在形美方面，使格式更多样化。因此，元曲把诗歌进一步推向通俗化、口语化、灵活化，为近现代的白话文学开辟了道路，可以说是中国新文化运动的一个重要源头。

许渊冲
2004年2月20日

元好问

人月圆

卜居外家东园

（一）

重冈已隔红尘断，村落更年丰。
移居要就，窗中远岫，舍后长松。
十年种木，一年种谷，都付儿童。
老夫惟有醒来明月，醉后清风。

（二）

玄都观里桃千树，花落水空流。
凭君莫问，清泾浊渭，去马来牛。
谢公扶病，羊昙挥涕，一醉都休。
古今几度生存华屋，零落山丘！

小圣乐

骤雨打新荷

（一）

绿叶阴浓，遍池亭水阁，偏趁凉多。
海榴初绽，朵朵簇红罗。
乳燕雏莺弄语，有高柳鸣蝉相和。
骤雨过，珍珠乱撒，打遍新荷。

（二）

人生百年有几？念良辰美景，休放虚过！
穷通前定，何用苦张罗？
命友邀宾玩赏，对芳尊浅酌低歌。
且酩酊，任他两轮日月，来往如梭！

杨果

小桃红
采莲女

（一）

满城烟水月微茫，人倚兰舟唱。
常记相逢若耶上，隔三湘，碧云望断空惆怅。
美人笑道，莲花相似，情短藕丝长。

（二）

采莲湖上棹船回，风约湘裙翠。
一曲琵琶数行泪，望君归，芙蓉开尽无消息。
晚凉多少，红鸳白鹭，何处不双飞？

刘秉忠

干荷叶

（一）

干荷叶，色苍苍，老柄风摇荡。
减了清香越添黄。
都因昨夜一场霜，寂寞在秋江上。

（二）

干荷叶，色无多，不耐风霜剉。
贴秋波，倒枝柯。
官娃齐唱采莲歌，梦里繁华过。

（三）

南高峰，北高峰，惨淡烟霞洞。
宋高宗，一场空。
吴山依旧酒旗风，两度江南梦。

杜仁杰

耍孩儿
庄家不识构阑

（一）

风调雨顺民安乐，都不似俺庄家快活。
桑蚕五谷十分收，官司无甚差科。
当村许下还心愿，来到城中买些纸火。
正打街头过，见吊个花碌碌纸榜，
不似那答儿闹穰穰人多。

（二）六煞

见一个人手撑着椽做的门，高声的叫"请请！"
道"迟来的满了无处停坐"。
说道"前截儿院本《调风月》，
背后么末敷演刘耍和。"
高声叫："赶散易得，难得的妆哈。"

（三）五煞

要了二百钱放过咱，入得门上个木坡，
见层层叠叠团圞坐。
抬头觑是个钟楼模样，往下觑却是人旋窝。
见几个妇女向台儿上坐，
又不是迎神赛社，不住的擂鼓筛锣。

（四）四煞

一个女孩儿转了几遭，不多时引出一伙。
中间里一个央人货，裹着枚皂头巾
顶门上插一管笔，满脸石灰
更着些黑道儿抹。知他待是如何过？
浑身上下，则穿领花布直裰。

（五）三煞

念了会诗共词，说了会赋与歌，无差错。
唇天口地无高下，巧语花言记许多。
临绝末，道了低头撮脚，爨罢将么拨。

（六）二煞

一个妆做张太公，他改做小二哥，
行行行说向城中过。
见个年少的妇女，向帘儿下立。
那老子用意铺谋，待取做老婆。
教小二哥相撮合，但要的豆谷米麦，
问甚布绢纱罗。

(七)一煞

教太公往前挪,不敢往后挪,
抬左脚不敢抬右脚。翻来覆去由他一个。
太公心下实焦懆,把一个皮棒槌
则一下打做两半个。我则道脑袋天灵破,
则道兴词告状,刬地大笑呵呵。

(八)尾

则被一泡尿,爆的我没奈何。
刚揑刚忍更待看些儿个,枉被这驴颓笑杀我。

王和卿

醉中天

咏大蝴蝶

弹破庄周梦,两翅驾东风。
三百座名园,一采个空。
谁道风流种,唬杀寻芳的蜜蜂?
轻轻的飞动,把卖花人扇过桥东。

一半儿

题情

（一）
书来和泪怕开缄，又不归来空再三。
这样病儿谁惯耽！越恁瘦岩岩，
一半儿增添一半儿减。

（二）
将来书信手拈着，灯下恣恣观觑了。
两三行字真带草，提起来越心焦，
一半儿丝挦一半儿烧。

（三）
别来宽袒缕金衣，粉悴烟憔减玉肌。
泪点儿只除衫袖知，盼佳期，
一半儿才干一半儿湿。

盍西村

小桃红

江岸水灯

万家灯火闹春桥，十里光相照。
舞凤翔鸾势绝妙。可怜宵！波间涌出蓬莱岛。
香烟乱飘，笙歌喧闹，飞上玉楼腰。

小桃红
客船晚烟

绿云冉冉锁清湾,香彻东西岸。
官课今年九分办。厮追攀,渡头买得新鱼雁。
杯盘不干,欢欣无限,忘了大家难。

小桃红
杂咏

杏花开候不曾晴,败尽游人兴。
红雪飞来满芳径。问春莺,春莺无语风方定。
小蛮有情,夜凉人静,唱彻醉翁亭。

商挺

潘妃曲

带月披星担惊怕,久立纱窗下。
等候他。蓦听得门外地皮儿踏,
则道是冤家,原来风动荼蘼架。

胡祗遹

沉醉东风

渔樵

渔得鱼心满愿足,樵得樵眼笑眉舒。
一个罢了钓竿,一个收了斤斧。
林泉下偶然相遇,是两个不识字渔樵士大夫。
他两个笑加加的谈今论古。

伯颜

喜春来

金鱼玉带罗襕扣,皂盖朱幡列五侯。
山河判断在俺笔尖头。得意秋,分破帝王忧。

王恽

平湖乐

尧庙秋社

社坛烟淡散林鸦,把酒观多稼。
霹雳弦声斗高下,笑喧哗,壤歌亭外山如画。
朝来致有,西山爽气,不羡日夕佳。

卢挚

节节高
题洞庭鹿角庙壁

雨晴云散,满江明月。
风微浪息,扁舟一叶。
半夜心,三生梦,万里别。闷倚篷窗睡些。

沉醉东风
秋景

挂绝壁枯松倒倚,落残霞孤鹜齐飞。
四围不尽山,一望无穷水。
散西风满天秋意。
夜静云帆月影低,载我在潇湘画里。

沉醉东风
闲居

恰离了绿水青山那答,早来到竹篱茅舍人家。
野花路畔开,村酒槽头榨。
直吃的欠欠答答。
醉了山童不劝咱,白发上黄花乱插。

沉醉东风

春情

残花酿蜂儿蜜脾,细雨和燕子香泥。
白雪柳絮飞,红雨桃花坠。
杜鹃声又是春归。
纵有新诗赠别离,医不可相思病体。

蟾宫曲

扬州汪右丞席上即事

江城歌吹风流,雨过平山,月满西楼。
几许华年?三生醉梦,六月凉秋。
按锦瑟佳人劝酒,卷珠帘齐按凉州。
客去还留,云树萧萧,河汉悠悠。

蟾宫曲

醉赠乐府珠帘秀

系行舟谁遣卿卿?爱林下风姿,云外歌声。
宝髻堆云,冰弦散雨,总是才情。
恰绿树南熏晚晴,险些儿羞杀啼莺。
客散邮亭,楚调将成,醉梦初醒。

殿前欢

酒兴

酒杯浓，一葫芦春色醉山翁，
一葫芦酒压花梢重。
随我奚童，葫芦干，兴不穷。
谁人共？一带青山送。
乘风列子，列子乘风。

陈草庵

山坡羊

叹世

晨鸡初叫，昏鸦争噪，那个不去红尘闹？
路迢遥，水迢迢，功名尽在长安道。
今日少年明日老。
山，依旧好；人，憔悴了。

关汉卿

白鹤子

香焚金鸭鼎，闲傍小红楼。
月在柳梢头，人约黄昏后。

四块玉

别情

自送别,心难舍,一点相思几时绝?
凭阑袖拂梅花雪。
溪又斜,山又遮,人去也。

四块玉

闲适

(一)
意马收,心猿锁,跳出红尘恶风波。
淮阴午梦谁惊破?
离了利名场,钻入安乐窝,闲快活。

(二)
南亩耕,东山卧,世态人情经历多。
闲将往事思量过,
贤的是他,愚的是我,争甚么?

沉醉东风

送别

咫尺的天南地北,霎时间月缺花飞。
手执着饯行杯,眼阁着别离泪。
刚道得声保重将息,痛煞煞叫人舍不得。
好去者,望前程万里!

大德歌

（一）

谢家村，赏芳春。疑怪他桃花冷笑人。
着谁传芳信？强题诗也断魂，
花阴下等待无人问，只听得黄犬吠柴门。

（二）

风飘飘，雨潇潇。便做陈抟也睡不着。
懊恼伤怀抱。扑簌簌泪点抛。
秋蝉儿噪罢寒蛩儿叫，淅零零细雨打芭蕉。

碧玉箫

（一）

膝上琴横，哀愁动离情。
指下风生，潇洒弄清声。
锁窗前月色明，雕阑外夜气清。
指法轻，助起骚人兴。
听！正漏断，人初静。

（二）

席上尊前，衾枕奈无缘。
柳底花边，诗曲已多年。
向人前未敢言，自心中祷苍天。
情意坚，每日空相见。
天！甚时节，成姻眷？

一枝花

不伏老

（一）

攀出墙朵朵花，折临路枝枝柳。
花攀红蕊嫩，柳折翠条柔。浪子风流。
凭着我折柳攀花手，直熬得花残柳败休。
半生来折柳攀花，一世里眠花宿柳。

（二）梁州第七

我是个普天下郎君领袖，盖世界浪子班头。
愿朱颜不改常依旧，花中消遣，酒内忘忧；
分茶攧竹，打马藏阄。
通五音六律滑熟，甚闲愁到我心头？
伴的是银筝女，银台前理银筝笑倚银屏；
伴的是玉天仙，携玉手并玉肩同登玉楼；
伴的是金钗客，歌金缕捧金尊满泛金瓯。
你道我老也暂休，
占排场风月功名首，更玲珑又剔透。
我是个锦阵花营都帅头，曾玩府游州。

(三)隔尾

子弟每是个茅草岗沙土窝初生的兔羔儿
乍向围场上走,我是个经笼罩受索网
苍翎毛老野鸡蹅踏的阵马儿熟。
经了些窝弓冷箭铁枪头,不曾落人后。
恰不道人到中年万事休,我怎肯虚度了春秋?

(四)尾

我是个蒸不烂煮不熟捶不扁炒不爆响珰珰一粒铜豌豆。
恁子弟每谁教你钻入他
锄不断斫不下解不开顿不脱慢腾腾千层锦套头?
我玩的是梁园月,饮的是东京酒,
赏的是洛阳花,攀的是章台柳。
我也会吟诗,会篆籀,会弹丝,会品竹;
我也会唱鹧鸪,舞垂手,
会打围,会蹴踘,会围棋,会双陆。
你便是落了我牙,歪了我口,瘸了我腿,折了我手,
天赐与我这几般儿歹症候,尚兀自不肯休。
则除是阎王亲自唤,神鬼自来勾,
三魂归地府,七魄丧冥幽,
天哪,那其间才不向烟花路儿上走。

寄生草
饮

长醉后方何碍？不醒时有甚思？
糟腌两个功名字，醅渰千古兴亡事，
曲埋万丈虹蜺志。
不达时皆笑屈原非，但知音尽说陶潜是。

阳春曲
题情

轻拈斑管书心事，细折银笺写恨词。
可怜不惯害相思，则被你个肯字儿
迤逗我许多时。

天净沙
（一）春

春山暖日和风，阑干楼阁帘栊，杨柳秋千院中。
啼莺舞燕，小桥流水飞红。

（二）夏

云收雨过波添，楼高水冷瓜甜，绿树阴垂画檐。
纱幮藤簟，玉人罗扇轻缣。

（三）秋

孤村落日残霞，轻烟老树寒鸦，一点飞鸿影下。
青山绿水，白草红叶黄花。

（四）冬

一声画角樵门，半庭新月黄昏，雪里山前水滨。
竹篱茅舍，淡烟衰草孤村。

沉醉东风

渔夫

黄芦岸白蘋渡口，绿杨堤红蓼滩头。
虽无刎颈交，却有忘机友。
点秋江白鹭沙鸥，傲杀人间万户侯，
不识字烟波钓叟。

姚燧

醉高歌

感怀

十年书剑长吁，一曲琵琶暗许。
月明江上别湓浦，愁听兰舟夜雨。

凭阑人

寄征衣

欲寄君衣君不还,不寄君衣君又寒。
寄与不寄间,妾身千万难。

庾天锡

雁儿落过得胜令

(一) 雁儿落

从他绿鬓斑,欹枕白石烂。
回头红日晚,满目青山矸。

(二) 得胜令

翠立数峰寒,碧锁暮云间。
媚景春前赏,晴岚雨后看。
开颜,玉盏金波满。
狼山,人生相会难。

刘敏中

黑漆弩
村居遣兴

长巾阔领深村住,不识我唤作伧父。
掩白沙翠竹柴门,听彻秋来夜雨。
闲将得失思量,往事水流东去。
便宜教画却凌烟,甚是功名了处?

马致远

四块玉
浔阳江

送客时,秋江冷,商女琵琶断肠声。
可知道司马和愁听?
月又明,酒又醒,客乍醒。

四块玉
叹世

两鬓皤,中年过,图甚区区苦张罗?
人间宠辱都参破。
种春风二顷田,远红尘千丈波,倒大来闲快活。

天净沙

秋思

枯藤老树昏鸦,小桥流水人家,古道西风瘦马。
夕阳西下,断肠人在天涯。

清江引

野兴

(一)

绿蓑衣紫罗袍谁是主?两件儿都无济。
便作钓鱼人,也在风波里。
则不如寻个稳便处,闲坐地。

(二)

林泉隐居谁到此?有客清风至。
会作山中相,不管人间事。
争甚么半张名利纸?

寿阳曲

(一)山市晴岚

花村外,草店西,晚霞明雨收天霁。
四围山一竿残照里,锦屏风又添铺翠。

(二)远浦帆归

夕阳下,酒旆闲,两三航未曾着岸。
落花水香茅舍晚,断桥头卖鱼人散。

(三)潇湘夜雨

渔灯暗,客梦回,一声声滴人心碎。
孤舟五更家万里,是离人几行情泪。

寿阳曲

从别后,音信绝,薄情种害煞人也。
逢一个见一个因话说,不信你耳轮儿不热。

秋思

(一)夜行船

百岁光阴一梦蝶,重回首往事堪嗟。
今日春来,明朝花谢。
急罚盏夜阑灯灭。

（二）乔木查

想秦官汉阙，都做了衰草牛羊野。
不恁么渔樵没话说。
纵荒坟横断碑，不辨龙蛇。

（三）庆宣和

投至狐踪与兔穴，多少豪杰！
鼎足虽坚半腰里折。魏耶？晋耶？

（四）落梅风

天教你富，莫太奢！没多时好天良夜。
富家儿更做道你心似铁，争辜负了锦堂风月！

（五）风入松

眼前红日又西斜，疾似下坡车。
不争镜里添白雪，上床与鞋履相别。
休笑巢鸠计拙，葫芦提一向装呆。

（六）拨不断

利名竭，是非绝。
红尘不向门前惹，绿树偏宜屋角遮，
青山争补墙头缺。
更那堪竹篱茅舍！

(七)离亭宴煞

蛩吟罢一觉才宁贴,鸡鸣时万事无休歇,
争名利何时是彻!
看密匝匝蚁排兵,乱纷纷蜂酿蜜,急攘攘蝇争血。
裴公绿野堂,陶令白莲社。
爱秋来时那些:
和露摘黄花,带霜烹紫蟹,煮酒烧红叶。
想人生有限杯,浑几个重阳节。
嘱咐你个顽童记者,便北海探吾来,道东篱醉了也。

赵孟頫

后庭花

秋思

清溪一叶舟,芙蓉两岸秋。
采菱谁家女?歌声起暮鸥。
乱云愁,满头风雨,戴荷叶归去休。

王实甫

十二月过尧民歌

别情

（一）十二月

自别后遥山隐隐，更那堪远水粼粼？
见杨柳飞绵滚滚；对桃花醉脸醺醺。
透内阁香风阵阵；掩重门暮雨纷纷。

（二）尧民歌

怕黄昏忽地又黄昏；不销魂怎地不销魂？
新啼痕压旧啼痕；断肠人忆断肠人。
今春，香肌瘦几分；裙带宽三寸。

滕宾

普天乐

翠荷残，苍梧坠。千山应瘦，万木皆稀。
蜗角名，蝇头利，输与渊明陶陶醉。
尽黄菊围绕东篱，良田数顷，黄牛二只，归去来兮！

邓玉宾

叨叨令
道情(一)

白云深处青山下,茅庵草舍无冬夏。
闲来几句渔樵话,困来一枕葫芦架。
你省的也么哥,你省的也么哥?
煞强如风波千丈,担惊怕。

叨叨令
道情(二)

一个空皮囊,包裹着千重气;
一个干骷髅,顶戴着十分罪。
为儿女使尽些拖刀计;
为家私费尽些担山力。
你省的也么哥,你省的也么哥?
这一个长生道理何人会?

殿前欢

懒云窝

懒云窝,醒时诗酒醉时歌。
瑶琴不理抛书卧,无梦南柯。得清闲尽快活。
日月似撺梭过,富贵比花开落。
青春去也,不乐如何?

冯子振

鹦鹉曲

山亭逸兴

嵯峨峰顶移家住,是个不唧溜樵父。
烂柯时树老无花,叶叶枝枝风雨。
故人曾唤我归来,却道不如休去。
指门前万叠云山,是不费青蚨买处。

鹦鹉曲

别意

花骢嘶断留侬住,满酌酒劝据鞍父。
柳青青万里初程,点染阳关朝雨。
怨春风雁不回头,一个个背人飞去。
望河桥敛衽频啼,早蓦到长亭短处。

珠帘秀

寿阳曲
答卢疏斋

山无数,烟万缕,憔悴煞玉堂人物。
倚蓬窗一身儿活受苦。恨不得随大江东去!

贯云石

塞鸿秋
代人作

战西风几点宾鸿至,感起我南朝千古伤心事。
展花笺欲写几句知心事,
空教我停霜毫半晌无才思。
往常得兴时,一扫无瑕疵。
今日个病厌厌,刚写下两个相思字。

红绣鞋

挨着靠着云窗同坐,偎着抱着月枕双歌,
听着数着愁着怕着早四更过。
四更过情未足,情未足夜如梭。
天哪,更闰一更儿妨甚么!

落梅风

新秋至,人乍别,顺长江水流残月。
悠悠画船东去也,这思量起头儿一夜。

蟾宫曲

送春

问东君何处天涯?落日啼鹃,流水桃花。
淡淡遥山,萋萋芳草,隐隐残霞。
随柳絮吹归那答,趁游丝惹在谁家?
倦理琵琶,人倚秋千,月照窗纱。

清江引

咏梅

南枝夜来先破蕊,泄漏春消息。
偏宜雪月交,不惹蜂蝶戏。
有时节暗香来梦里。

张养浩

得胜令
四月一日喜雨

万象欲焦枯,一雨足沾濡。
天地回生意,风雨起壮图。
农夫,舞破蓑衣绿;
和余,欢喜的无是处。

水仙子

中年才过便休官,合共神仙一样看。
出门来山水相留恋,倒大来耳根清眼界宽,
细寻思这的是真欢。
黄金带缠着忧患,紫罗襕裹着祸端。
怎如俺藜杖藤冠?

山坡羊
潼关怀古

峰峦如聚,波涛如怒,山河表里潼关路。
望西都,意踟蹰。
伤心秦汉经行处,宫阙万间都做了土。
兴,百姓苦;亡,百姓苦。

朝天子

柳堤,竹溪,日影筛金翠。
杖藜徐步近钓矶,看鸥鹭闲游戏。
农父渔翁,贪营活计,不知他在图画里。
对着这般景致,坐的,便无酒也令人醉。

白贲

鹦鹉曲

侬家鹦鹉洲边住,是个不识字渔父。
浪花中一叶扁舟,睡煞江南烟雨。
觉来时满眼青山,抖擞绿蓑归去。
算从前错怨天公,甚也有安排我处。

郑光祖

蟾宫曲

(一)

弊裘尘土压征鞍,鞭倦袅芦花。
弓剑萧萧,一竟入烟霞。
动羁怀,西风禾黍,秋水兼葭。
千点万点老树寒鸦,
三行两行写高寒,呀呀雁落平沙。

(二)

曲岸西边近水涡。鱼网纶竿钓艖 。
断桥东下傍溪沙，疏篱茅舍人家。
见满山满谷，红叶黄花。
正是凄凉时候，离人又在天涯。

曾瑞

骂玉郎过感皇恩采茶歌
闺中闻杜鹃

(一) 骂玉郎

无情杜宇闲淘气，头直上耳根底，声声聒得人心碎。
你怎知，我就里，愁无际？

(二) 感皇恩

帘幕低垂，重门深闭。
曲阑边，雕檐外，画楼西。
把春醒唤起，将晓梦惊回。
无明夜，闲聒噪，厮禁持。

(三) 采茶歌

我几曾离这绣罗帏？没来由劝我道"不如归"！
江南正着迷，这声儿，好去对俺那人啼。

集贤宾
宫词

(一)

闷登楼倚阑干,看暮景,天阔水云平。
浸池面楼台倒影,书云笺雁字斜横。
衰柳拂月户云窗,残荷临水阁凉亭。
景凄凉助人愁越逞,下妆楼步月空庭。
乌惊环佩响,鹤吹铎铃鸣。

(二)逍遥乐

对景如青鸾舞镜,天隔羊车,人囚凤城。
好姻缘辜负了今生,痛伤悲雨泪如倾。
心如醉满怀何日醒?西风传玉漏丁宁。
恰过半夜,胜似三秋,才交四更。

(三)金菊香

秋虫夜语不堪听,啼树宫鸦不住声。
入孤帏强眠寻梦境,被相思鬼绰了魂灵,
纵有梦也难成。

(四)醋葫芦

睡不着,坐不宁,又不疼不痛病萦萦。
待不思量雯儿,心未肯,没乱到更阑人静。

（五）高平煞

照愁人残蜡碧荧荧，沉水烟消金兽鼎。
败叶走庭除，修竹扫苍楹。
唱道是人和闷可难争。
则我瘦身躯怎敢共愁肠竞？
伤心情脉脉，病体困腾腾。
画屋风轻，翠被寒增，也温不过早来袜儿冷。

（六）尾

睡魔盼不来，丫鬟叫不应，香消烛灭冷清清。
唯嫦娥与人无世情，可怜咱孤另，
透疏帘斜照月偏明。

睢景臣

哨遍

高祖还乡

（一）

社长排门告示，但有的差使无推故。
这差使不寻俗：一壁厢纳草除根，
一边又要差夫，索应付。
又言是车驾，都说是銮舆，今日还乡故。
王乡老执定瓦台盘，赵忙郎抱着酒葫芦。
新刷来的头巾，恰糨来的绸衫，畅好是妆幺大户。

（二）耍孩儿

瞎王留引定火乔男女，胡踢蹬吹笛擂鼓。
见一彪人马到庄门，劈头里几面旗舒。
一面旗白胡阑套住个迎霜兔
一面旗红曲连打着个毕月乌。
一面旗鸡学舞，一面旗狗生双翅，
一面旗蛇缠葫芦。

（三）五煞

红漆了叉，银铮了斧，甜瓜苦瓜黄金镀。
明晃晃马镫枪尖上挑，白雪雪鹅毛扇上铺。
这几个乔人物，拿着些不曾见的器仗，
穿着些大作怪衣服。

（四）四煞

辕条上都是马，套顶上不见驴，黄罗伞柄天生曲。
车前八个天曹判，车后若干递送夫。
更几个多娇女，一般穿著，一样妆梳。

（五）三煞

那大汉下的车，众人施礼数。
那大汉觑得人如无物。
众乡老展脚舒腰拜，那大汉挪身着手扶。
猛可里抬头觑，觑多时认得，险气破我胸脯。

(六)二煞

你身须姓刘,你妻须姓吕。
把你两家儿根脚从头数。
你本身做亭长耽几盏酒,你丈人教村学读几卷书。
曾在俺庄东住,也曾与我喂牛切草,拽坝扶锄。

(七)一煞

春采了桑,冬借了俺粟。零支了米麦无重数。
换田契强秤了麻三秤,还酒债偷量了豆几斛。
有甚胡涂处?明标着册历,现放着文书。

(八)尾声

少我的钱差发内旋拨还,
欠我的粟税粮中私准除。
只道刘三,谁肯把你揪摔住?
白甚么改了姓更了名,唤做汉高祖!

周文质

叨叨令

悲秋

叮叮当当铁马儿乞留玎琅闹,
啾啾唧唧促织儿依柔依然叫。
滴滴点点细雨儿淅零淅留哨,
潇潇洒洒梧叶儿失流疏剌落。
睡不着也末哥,睡不着也末哥,
孤孤另另单枕上迷彪模登靠。

塞儿令

挑短檠,倚云屏,伤心伴人清瘦影。
薄酒初醒,好梦难成,斜月为谁明?
闷恹恹听彻残更,意迟迟盼杀多情。
西风穿户冷,檐马隔帘鸣。
叮,疑是佩环声。

乔吉

清江引

有感

相思瘦因人间阻,只隔墙儿住。
笔尖和露珠,花瓣题诗句,
倩衔泥燕儿将过去。

清江引

即景

垂杨翠丝千万缕,惹住闲情绪。
和泪送春归,倩水将愁去,
是溪边落红昨夜雨。

山坡羊

冬日写怀

(一)
朝三暮四,昨非今是。痴儿不解荣枯事。
攒家私,宠花枝,黄金壮起荒淫志,
千百锭买张招状纸。
身,已至此;心,犹未死。

(二)
离家一月,闲居客舍,孟尝君不费黄齑社。
世情别,故交绝,床头金尽谁行借?
今日又逢冬至节。
酒,何处赊?梅,何处折?

(三)
冬寒前后,雪晴时候,谁人相伴梅花瘦?
钓鳌舟,缆汀洲,绿蓑不耐风霜透。
投至有鱼来上钩,
风,吹破头;霜,皴破手。

卖花声
悟世

肝肠百炼炉间铁,富贵三更枕上蝶,
功名两字酒中蛇。
尖风薄雪,残杯冷炙,掩青灯竹篱茅舍。

凭阑人
春思

淡月梨花曲槛旁,清露苍苔罗袜凉。
恨他愁断肠,为他烧夜香。

凭阑人
小姬

手拈红牙花满头,爱唱春词不解愁。
一声出画楼,晓莺无奈羞。

凭阑人
金陵道中

瘦马驮诗天一涯,倦鸟呼愁村数家。
扑头飞柳花,与人添鬓华。

折桂令

毗陵晚眺

江南倦客登临，多少豪雄，几许消沉？
今日何堪，买田阳羡，挂剑长林？
霞缕烂谁家昼锦？月钩横故国丹心。
窗影灯深，磷火青青，山鬼喑喑。

折桂令

登毗陵永庆阁所见

忽飞来南浦娇云，背影藏羞，忍笑含颦。
绕鬓兰烟，沾衣花气，恼梦梅魂。
似湘水行春洛神，遇天台采药刘晨。
愁缕成痕，一枕余香，半醉黄昏。

折桂令

客窗清明

风风雨雨梨花，窄索帘栊，巧小窗纱。
甚情绪灯前，客怀枕畔，心事天涯！
三千丈清霜鬓发，五十年春梦繁华。
蓦见人家，杨柳分烟，扶上檐牙。

折桂令

荆溪即事

问荆溪溪上人家,为甚人家,不种梅花?
老树支门,荒蒲绕岸,苦竹圈笆。
寺无僧狐狸样瓦,官无事乌鼠当衙。
白水黄沙,倚遍阑干,数尽啼鸦。

满庭芳

渔父词

(一)
携鱼换酒,鱼鲜可口,酒热扶头。
盘中不是鲸鲵肉,鲟鲊初熟。
太湖水光摇酒瓯,洞庭山影落鱼舟。
归来后,一竿钓钩,不挂古今愁。

(二)
江声撼枕,一川残月,满目遥岑。
白云流水无人禁,胜似山林。
钓晚霞寒波濯锦,看秋潮夜海熔金。
村醪窨,何人共饮?鸥鹭是知心。

殿前欢

登江山第一楼

拍阑干,雾花吹鬓海风寒,浩歌惊得浮云散。
细数青山,指蓬莱一望间。
纱巾岸,鹤背骑来惯。
举头长啸,直上天坛。

小桃红

效联珠格

落花飞絮隔朱帘,帘静重门掩。
掩镜羞看脸儿䩞,䩞眉尖,眉尖指屈将归期念。
念他抛闪,闪咱少欠,欠你病恹恹。

水仙子

寻梅

冬前冬后几村庄,溪北溪南两履霜,
树头树底孤山上。
冷风来何处香?忽相逢缟袂绡裳。
酒醒寒惊梦,笛凄春断肠,淡月昏黄。

水仙子

为友人作

搅柔肠离恨病相兼,重聚首佳期卦怎占?
豫章城开了座相思店。
闷勾肆儿逐日添,愁行货顿塌在眉尖。
税钱比茶船上欠,斤两去等秤上掂,
吃紧的历册般拘钤。

雁儿落过得胜令

忆别

(一)雁儿落

殷勤红叶诗,冷淡黄花市。
清江天水笺,白雁云烟字。

(二)得胜令

游子去何之?无处寄新词。
酒醒灯昏夜,窗寒梦觉时。
寻思,谈笑十年事;
嗟咨,风流两鬓丝。

集贤宾
咏柳忆别

（一）

恨青青画桥东畔柳，曾相送少年游。
散晴雪杨花清昼，又一场心事悠悠。
翠丝长不系雕鞍，碧云寒空掩珠楼。
揎罗袖试将纤玉手，绾东风摇损轻柔。
同心方胜结，缨络绣文毬。

（二）逍遥乐

绾不成鸳鸯双扣，空惊散梢头，一双锦鸠。
何处忘忧？
听枝上数声黄栗留，怕不弄春娇巧啭歌喉？
惊回好梦，题起离情，唤醒闲愁。

（三）醋葫芦

雨晴珠泪收，烟罨翠黛羞。殢风流还自怨风流。
病多不奈秋，未秋来早先消瘦。晓风残月在帘钩。

（四）浪里来煞

不要你护雕阑花甃香，荫苍苍石径幽。
只要你盼行人终日替我凝眸。
只要你重温灞陵别后酒。
如今时候，只要向绿阴深处缆归舟。

刘时中

殿前欢

醉颜酡,太翁庄上走如梭。
门前几个官人坐,有虎皮驮驮。
呼王留唤伴哥,无一个,空叫得喉咙破。
人踏了瓜果,马践了田禾。

阿鲁威

落梅风

千年志,一旦空。惟有纸钱灰晚风吹送。
尽蜀鹃血啼烟树中,唤不回一场春梦。

王元鼎

醉太平

寒食

声声啼乳鸦,生叫破韶华。
夜深微雨润堤沙,香风万家。
画楼洗尽鸳鸯瓦,彩绳半湿秋千架。
觉来红日上窗纱,听街头卖杏花。

薛昂夫

塞鸿秋

功名万里忙如燕,斯文一脉微如线。
光阴寸隙流如电,风霜两鬓白如练。
尽道便休官,林下何曾见?至今寂寞彭泽县。

楚天遥过清江引

送春

(一)楚天遥

有意送春归,无计留春住。明年又春来,何似休归去?
桃花也解愁,点点飘红玉。目断楚天遥,不见春归路。

(二)清江引

春若有情春更苦,暗里韶光度。
夕阳山外山,春水渡傍渡。不知那答儿春住处。

吴弘道

金字经

(一)

落花风飞去,故枝依旧鲜。月缺终须有再圆。
圆,月圆人未圆。朱颜变,几时得重少年?

金字经

(二)

这家春醪尽,那家酷瓮开。卖了肩头一担柴。
哈!酒钱怀内揣。葫芦在,大家提去来。

拨不断

闲乐

(一)

泛浮槎,寄生涯,长江万里秋风驾。
稚子和烟煮嫩茶,老妻带月包新鲊,醉时闲话。

(二)

利名无,宦情疏,彭泽升斗微官禄。
蠹鱼食残架上书,晓霜荒尽篱边菊,罢官归去。

赵善庆

折桂令
湖山堂

八窗开水月交光,诗酒坛台,莺燕排场。
歌扇摇风,梨云飘雪,粉黛生香。
红烛台已更旧邦,白头民犹说新堂。
花妒幽芳,人换宫妆。惟有湖山不管兴亡。

沉醉东风
秋日湘阴道中

山对面蓝堆翠岫,草齐腰绿染沙洲。
傲霜橘柚青,濯雨蒹葭秀。
隔沧波隐隐江楼。
点破潇湘万顷秋,是几叶儿传黄败柳。

庆东原
泊罗阳驿

砧声住,蛩韵切,静寥寥门掩清秋夜。
秋心凤阙,秋愁雁堞,秋梦蝴蝶。
十载故乡心,一夜邮亭月。

马谦斋

柳营曲
太平即事

亲凤塔,住龙沙,天下太平无事也。
辞却公衙,别了京华,甘分老农家。
傲河阳潘岳栽花,效东门邵平种瓜。
庄前栽果木,山下种桑麻。
度岁华,活计老生涯。

张可久

人月圆
山中书事

兴亡千古繁华梦,诗眼倦天涯。
孔林乔木,吴官蔓草,楚庙寒鸦。
数间茅舍,藏书万卷,投老村家。
山中何事?松花酿酒,春水煎茶。

人月圆
春晚次韵

萋萋芳草春云乱,愁在夕阳中。
短亭别酒,平湖画舫,垂柳骄骢。
一声啼鸟,一番夜雨,一阵东风。
桃花吹尽,佳人何在?门掩残红。

人月圆

春日湖上

小楼还被青山碍,隔断楚天遥。
昨宵入梦,那人如玉,何处吹箫?
门前朝暮,无情秋月,有信春潮。
看看憔悴,飞花心事,残柳眉梢。

醉太平

怀古

翩翩野舟,泛泛沙鸥,登临不尽古今愁。白云去留。
凤凰台上青山旧,秋千墙里垂杨瘦,
琵琶亭畔野花秋,长江自流。

醉太平

感怀

人皆嫌命窘,谁不见钱亲?
水晶环入面糊盆,才沾粘便滚。
文章糊了盛钱囤,门廊改做迷魂阵,
清廉贬入睡馄饨,葫芦提倒稳。

锦橙梅

红馥馥的脸衬霞，黑髭髭的鬓堆鸦。
料应他，必是个中人，打扮的堪描画。
颤巍巍的插着翠花，宽绰绰的穿着轻纱。
兀的不风韵煞人也嗏。
是谁家？我不住了偷睛儿抹。

迎仙客

秋夜

雨乍晴，月笼明，秋香院落砧杵鸣。
二三更，千万声，捣碎离情，不管愁人听。

红绣鞋

宁元帅席上

鸣玉佩凌烟图画，乐云村投老生涯。
少年谁识故侯家？
青蛇昏宝剑，团锦碎袍花，飞龙闲厩马。

红绣鞋

虎丘道上

船系谁家古岸？人归何处青山？
且将诗做图画看：
雁声芦叶老，鹭影蓼花寒，鹤巢松树晚。

梧叶儿

湖山夜景

猿啸黄昏后,人行画卷中。
萧寺罢疏钟,湿翠横千嶂,清风响万松。
寒玉奏孤桐,身在秋香月宫。

梧叶儿

有所思

人何处?草自春,弦索已生尘。
柳线萦离思,荷衣拭泪痕。
梅屋锁吟魂,目断吴山暮云。

折桂令

西陵送别

画船儿载不起离愁,人到西陵,恨满东州。
懒上归鞍,慵开泪眼,怕倚层楼。
春去春来,管送别依依岸柳;
潮生潮落,会忘机泛泛沙鸥。
烟水悠悠,有句相酬,无计相留。

折桂令

九日

对青山强整乌纱,归雁横秋,倦客思家。
翠袖殷勤,金杯错落,玉手琵琶。
人老去西风白发,蝶愁来明日黄花。
回首天涯,一抹斜阳,数点寒鸦。

折桂令

次韵

唤西施伴我西游,客路依依,烟水悠悠。
翠树啼鹃,青天旅雁,白雪盟鸥。
人倚梨花病酒,月明杨柳维舟。
试上层楼,绿满江南,红褪春愁。

折桂令

村庵即事

掩柴门啸傲烟霞,隐隐林峦,小小仙家。
楼外白云,窗前翠竹,井底朱砂。
五亩宅无人种瓜,一村庵有客分茶。
春色无多,开到蔷薇,落尽梨花。

水仙子

梅边即事

好花多向雨中开,佳客新从云外来。
清诗未了年前债,相逢且放怀。
曲阑干碾玉亭台,
小树纷蝶翅,苍苔点鹿胎,踏碎青鞋。

小桃红

离情

几场秋雨老黄花,不管离人怕。
一曲哀弦泪双下,放琵琶。
挑灯羞看围屏画,
声悲玉马,愁新罗帕,恨不到天涯。

普天乐

西湖即事

蕊珠宫,蓬莱洞。
青松影里,红藕香中。
千机云锦重,一片银河冻。
缥缈佳人双飞凤,紫箫寒月满长空。
阑干晚风,菱歌上下,渔火西东。

普天乐

秋怀

会真诗,相思债。
花笺象管,钿盒金钗。
雁啼明月中,人在青山外。
独上危楼愁无奈,起西风一片离怀。
白衣未来,东篱好在,黄菊先开。

喜春来

金华客舍

落红小雨苍苔径,飞絮东风细柳营,
可怜客里过清明。
不待听,昨夜杜鹃声。

喜春来

永康驿中

荷盘敲雨珠千颗,山背披云玉一梭,
半篇诗景费吟哦。
芳草坡,松外采茶歌。

朝天子

闺情

与谁画眉?猜破风流谜。
铜驼巷里玉骢嘶,夜半归来醉。
小意收拾,怪胆矜持,不识羞谁似你?
自知理亏,灯下和衣睡。

山坡羊

闺思

云松罗髻,香温鸳被,掩春闺一觉伤春睡。
柳花飞,小琼姬,一声雪下呈祥瑞。
团圆梦儿生唤起。
谁?不做美?呸,却是你!

殿前欢

离思

月笼沙,十年心事付琵琶。
相思懒看帏屏画,人在天涯。
春残豆蔻花,情寄鸳鸯帕,香冷荼蘼架。
旧游台榭,晓梦窗纱。

清江引

秋怀

西风信来家万里,问我归期未。
雁啼红叶天,人醉黄花地,
芭蕉雨声秋梦里。

天净沙

鲁卿庵中

青苔古木萧萧,苍云秋水迢迢,红叶山斋小小。
有谁曾到?探梅人过溪桥。

凭阑人

江夜

江水澄澄江月明,江上何人挡玉筝?
隔江和泪听,满江长叹声。

一枝花
湖上归

（一）

长天落彩霞，远水涵秋镜。
花如人面红，山似佛头青。
生色围屏，翠冷松云径，嫣然眉黛横。
但携将旖旎浓香，何必赋横斜瘦影？

（二）梁州

挽玉手留连锦英，据胡床指点银屏。
素娥不嫁伤孤另。
向当年小小，问何处卿卿？
东坡才调，西子娉婷，总相宜千古留名。
吾二人此地私行，六一泉亭上诗成。
三五夜花前月明，十四弦指下风生。
可憎，有情，捧红牙合和伊州令。
万籁寂，四山静，
幽咽泉流水下声，鹤怨猿惊。

（三）尾

岩阿禅窟鸣金磬，波底龙宫漾水精。
夜气清，酒力醒，宝篆销，玉漏鸣。
笑归来仿佛二更，煞强似踏雪寻梅，灞桥冷。

普天乐

垂虹夜月

玉华寒,冰壶冻。
云间玉兔,水面苍龙。
酒一樽,琴三弄,
唤起凌波仙人梦,倚阑干满面天风。
楼台远近,乾坤表里,江汉西东。

喜春来

皇亭夜泊

水深水浅东西涧,云去云来远近山,
秋风征棹钓鱼滩。
烟树晚,茅舍两三间。

蟾宫曲

江淹寺

紫霜毫是是非非。万古虚名,一梦初回。
失又何愁?得之何喜?闷也何为?
落日外萧山翠微,小桥边古寺残碑。
文藻珠玑,醉墨淋漓。
何似班超,投却毛锥?

蟾宫曲

春情

生平不会相思,才会相思,便害相思。
身似浮云,心如飞絮,气若游丝。
空一缕余香在此,盼千金游子何之?
证候来时,正是何时?
灯半昏时,月半明时。

水仙子

夜雨

一声梧叶一声秋,一点芭蕉一点愁,
三更归梦三更后。
落灯花棋未收,叹新丰孤馆人留。
枕上十年事,江南二老忧,都到心头。

水仙子

春情

九分恩爱九分忧,两处相思两处愁,
十年迤逗十年受。
几遍成几遍休,半点事半点惭羞。
三秋恨三秋感旧,三春怨三春病酒,
一世害一世风流。

人月圆

甘露怀古

江皋楼观前朝寺,秋色入秦淮。
败垣芳草,空廊落叶,深砌苍苔。
远人南去,夕阳西下,江水东来。
木兰花在,山僧试问,知为谁开?

朝天子

西湖

里湖,外湖,无处是无春处。
真山真水真画图,一片玲珑玉。
宜酒宜诗,宜晴宜雨。
销金锅,锦绣窟,
老苏,老逋,杨柳堤梅花墓。

查德卿

一半儿

春妆

自将杨柳品题人,笑拈花枝比较春。
输与海棠三四分,再偷匀,
一半儿胭脂一半儿粉。

柳营曲
金陵故址

临故国,认残碑,伤心六朝如逝水。
物换星移,城是人非,今古一枰棋。
南柯梦一觉初回,北邙坟三尺荒堆。
四围山护绕,几处树高低。
谁,曾赋黍离离?

唐毅夫

一枝花
怨雪

(一)

不呈六出祥,岂应三白瑞?
易添身上冷,能使腹中饥。
有甚稀奇?无主向沿街坠,不着人到处飞。
暗敲窗有影无形,偷入户潜踪蹑迹。

(二) 梁州

才苦上茅庵草舍,又钻入破壁疏篱,
似杨花滚滚轻狂势。
你几曾见贵公子锦裯绣褥?

你多曾伴老渔翁箬笠蓑衣?
为飘风胡做胡为,怕腾云相趁相随。
只着你冻的个孟浩然挣挣痴痴,
只着你逼的个林和靖钦钦历历,
只着你阻的个韩退之哭哭啼啼。
更长,漏迟,被窝中无半点儿阳和气。
恼人眠,搅人睡,
你那冷燥皮肤似铁石,着我怎敢相偎?

(三)尾

一冬酒债因他累,千里关山被你迷。
似这等浪蕊闲花,也不是长久计。
尽飘零数日,扫除做一堆,
我将你温不热薄情,化做了水。

朱庭玉

天净沙

秋

庭前落尽梧桐,水边开彻芙蓉。
解与诗人意同,辞柯霜叶,飞来就我题红。

张鸣善

普天乐
咏世

洛阳花,梁园月,好花须买,皓月须赊。
花倚栏杆看烂漫开,月曾把酒问团圆夜。
月有盈亏花有开谢,想人生最苦离别。
花谢了三春近也,月缺了中秋到也,
人去了何日来也?

普天乐
愁怀

雨儿飘,风儿飏。风吹回好梦,雨滴损柔肠。
风萧萧梧叶中,雨点点芭蕉上。
风雨相留添悲怆,雨和风卷起凄凉。
风雨儿怎当?风雨儿定当,风雨儿难当!

普天乐
嘲西席

讲诗书,习功课。
爹娘行孝顺,兄弟行谦和。
为臣要尽忠,与朋友休言过。
养性终朝端然坐,免教人笑俺风魔。
先生道学生琢磨,学生道先生絮聒,
馆东道不识字由他。

杨朝英

水仙子

西湖探梅

雪晴天地一冰壶，竟往西湖探老逋，
骑驴踏雪溪桥路。
笑王维作画图，拣梅花多处提壶。
对酒看花笑，无钱当剑沽，醉倒在西湖。

宋方壶

山坡羊

道情

青山相待，白云相爱，梦不到紫罗袍共黄金带。
一茅斋，野花开，
管甚谁家兴废谁成败？陋巷箪瓢亦乐哉！
贫，气不改；达，志不改。

清江引

托咏

剔秃圞一轮天外月，拜了低低说：
是必常团圆，休着些儿缺。
愿天下有情底都似你者。

斗鹌鹑
送别

（一）

落日遥岑，淡烟远浦。
萧寺疏钟，戍楼暮鼓。
一叶扁舟，数声去橹。
那惨戚，那凄楚，
恰待欢娱，顿成间阻。

（二）紫花儿

瘦岩岩香消玉减，冷清清夜永更长，
孤另另枕剩衾余。
羞花闭月，落雁沉鱼。
踌躇，从今后谁送萧娘一纸书？
无情无绪，水潪蓝桥，梦断华胥。

（三）调笑令

肺腑，恨怎舒？三叠阳关愁万缕，
幽期密约欢爱处，动离愁暮云无数。
今夜月明何处宿？依依古岸黄芦。

（四）秃厮儿

欢笑地不堪举目，回首处景物萧疏。
屋前月下谁共语？漫嗟吁，何如？

（五）圣药王

别太速，情最苦。
松金减玉瘦了身躯。
鬼病添，神思虚，
心如刀剜泪如珠，意儿里懒上香车。

（六）尾

眼睁睁怎忍分飞去？痛杀我也吹箫伴侣。
不付能恰住了送行客一帆风，又添起助离愁半江雨。

贾固

醉高歌过红绣鞋
寄金莺儿

（一）醉高歌

乐心儿比目连枝，肯意儿新婚燕尔。
画船开抛闪的人独自，遥望关西店儿。
黄河水流不尽心事，中条山隔不断相思。

（二）红绣鞋

当记得夜深沉，人静悄，自来时。
来时节三两句话，去时节一篇诗，
记在人心窝儿里直到死。

周德清

塞鸿秋
浔阳即景

长江万里自如练,淮山数点青如靛。
江帆几片疾如箭,山泉千尺飞如电。
晚云都变露,新月初学扇,塞鸿一字来如线。

满庭芳
看岳王传

披文握武,建中兴庙宇,载青史图书。
功成却被权臣妒,正落奸谋。
闪杀人望旌节中原士夫;
误杀人弃丘陵南渡銮舆。
钱塘路,愁风怨雨,长是洒西湖。

折桂令

倚蓬窗无语嗟呀,七件儿全无,做甚么人家?
柴似灵芝,油如甘露,米若丹砂。
酱瓮儿才罄撒,盐瓶儿又告消乏。
茶也无多,醋也无多。
七件事尚且艰难,怎生教我折柳攀花!

一枝花
秋夜闻筝

（一）

透疏帘风摇杨柳阴，泻长空月转梧桐影。
冷雕盘香销金兽火，咽铜龙漏滴玉壶冰。
何处银筝？声嘹呖云霄应，逐轻风过短棂，
耳才闻天上仙韶，身疑在人间胜境。

（二）梁州

恰便似溅石窟寒泉乱涌，集瑶台鸾凤和鸣，
走金盘乱撒骊珠迸。
嘶风骏偃，潜沼鱼惊。天边雁落，树梢云停。
早则是字样分明，更那堪音律关情？
凄凉比汉昭君塞上琵琶，
清韵如王子乔风前玉笙，悠扬似张君瑞月下琴声。
再听，愈惊。叮咛一曲阳关令。
感离愁，动别兴。万事萦怀百样增，一洗尘清。

（三）尾

他那里轻笼纤指冰弦应，
俺这里漫写花笺锦字迎。
越感起文园少年病。
是谁家玉卿？只恁般可憎！
唤的人一枕蝴蝶梦儿醒。

汪元亨

醉太平
警世

憎苍蝇竞血,恶黑蚁争穴。
急流中勇退是豪杰。不因循苟且,
叹乌衣一旦非王谢,怕青山两岸分吴越,
厌红尘万丈混龙蛇。老先生去也。

朝天子
归隐

荣华梦一场,功名纸半张,是非海波千丈。
马蹄踏碎禁街霜,听几度头鸡唱。
尘土衣冠,江湖心量,出皇家麟凤网。
慕夷齐首阳,叹韩彭未央,早纳纸风魔状。

沉醉东风
归田

远城市人稠物穰,近村居水色山光。
熏陶成野叟情,铲削去时官样,演习会牧歌樵唱。
老瓦盆边醉几场,不撞入天罗地网。

人月圆

惊回一枕当年梦,渔唱起南津。
画屏云嶂,池塘春草,无限销魂。
旧家应在,梧桐覆井,杨柳藏门。
闲身空老,孤篷听雨,灯火江村。

小桃红

一江秋水澹寒烟,水影明如练。眼底离愁数行雁。
雪晴天,绿树红蓼参差见。
吴歌荡桨,一声哀怨,惊起白鸥眠。

凭阑人

赠吴国良

客有吴郎吹洞箫,明月沉江春雾晓。
湘灵不可招,水云中环佩摇。

水仙子

东风花外小红楼,南浦山横眉黛愁。
春寒不管花枝瘦,无情水自流。
檐间燕语娇柔,惊回幽梦,
难寻旧游,落日帘钩。

刘庭信

折桂令
忆别

想人生最苦离别,唱到阳关,休唱三叠。
急煎煎抹泪柔眵,意迟迟揉腮擩耳,
呆答孩闭口藏舌。
情儿分儿你心里记者,病儿痛儿我身上添些。
家儿活儿既是抛撒,书儿信儿是必休绝,
花儿草儿打听的风声,车儿马儿我亲自来也!

水仙子
相思

恨重叠,重叠恨,恨绵绵,恨满晚妆楼。
愁积聚,积聚愁,愁切切,愁斟碧玉瓯。
懒梳妆,梳妆懒,懒设设,懒爇黄金兽。
泪珠弹,弹珠泪,泪汪汪,汪汪不住流。
病身躯,身躯病,病怏怏,病在我心头。
花见我,我见花,花应憔瘦。
月对咱,咱对月,月更害羞。
与天说,说与天,天也还愁。

一枝花

春日送别

丝丝杨柳风,点点梨花雨。
雨随花瓣落,风趁柳条疏。
春事成虚,无奈春归去。
春归何太速?试问东君,谁肯与莺花做主?

汤式

小梁州

九日渡江

(一)

秋风江上棹孤舟,烟水悠悠。
伤心无句赋登楼,山容瘦,老树替人愁。
(幺)
樽前醉把茱萸嗅,问相知几个白头?
乐可酬,人非旧,
黄花时候,难比旧风流。

(二)

秋风江上棹孤航,烟水茫茫。
白云西去雁南翔,推篷望,清思满沧浪。
(幺)
东篱载酒陶元亮,等闲间过了重阳。
自感伤,何情况,黄花惆怅,空作去年香。

天香引

忆维扬

羡江都自古神州,天上人间,楚尾吴头。
十万家画栋朱帘,百数曲红桥绿沼,
三千里锦缆龙舟。
柳招摇,花掩映,春风紫骝。
玉玎珰,珠络索,夜月香兜。
歌舞都休,光景难留。
富贵随落日西沉,繁华逐逝水东流。

兰楚芳

四块玉

风情

(一)

意思儿真,心肠儿顺。只争个口角头不囫囵。
怕人知,羞人说,嗔人问。
不见后又嗔,得见后又忖,多敢死后肯。

（二）

我事事村，他般般丑，丑则丑村则村意相投。
则为他丑心儿真，博得我村情儿厚。
似这般丑眷属，村配偶，只除天上有。

钟嗣成

醉太平
落魄

（一）

绕前街后街，进大院深宅。
怕有那慈悲好善小裙钗，
请乞儿一顿饱斋，与乞儿绣副合欢带，
与乞儿换副新铺盖，将乞儿携手上阳台。
救贫咱波奶奶！

（二）

风流贫最好，村沙富难交。
拾灰泥补砌了旧砖窑，开一个教乞儿市学，
裹一顶半新不旧乌纱帽，穿一领半长不短黄麻罩，
系一条半联不断皂环绦，做一个穷风月训导。

钱霖

哨遍

(一) 看钱奴

试把贤愚穷究,看钱奴自古呼铜臭。
徇己苦贪求,待不教泉货周流。
忍包羞,油铛插手,血海舒拳,肯落他人后?
晓夜寻思机彀,缘情钩距,巧取旁搜,
蝇头场上苦驱驰,马足尘中厮追逐,积攒下无厌就。
舍死忘生,出乖弄丑。

(二) 耍孩儿

安贫知足神明佑,好聚敛多招悔尤。
王戎遗下旧牙筹,夜连明计算无休。
不思日月搬乌兔,只与儿孙作马牛。
添消瘦,不调鼎鼐,恣逞戈矛。

(三) 十煞

渐消瘦双脸春,已凋飕两鬓秋。
终朝不乐眉长皱,恨不得
柜头钱五分息招人借,架上袄一周年不放赎。
狠毒心如狼狗,把平人骨肉,做自己膏油。

（四）九煞

有心待拜五侯，教人唤甚半州。
忍饥寒攒得家私厚。
待垒做钱山儿，倩军士喝号提铃守；
怕化做钱龙儿，请法官行罡布气留。
半炊儿八遍把牙关叩，只愿得无支有管，少出多收。

（五）八煞

亏心事尽量为，不义财尽力掊。
那里问亲弟兄亲姊妹亲姑舅。
只待要春风金谷骄王恺，一任教夜雨新丰困马周。
无亲旧，只知敬明眸皓齿，不想共肥马轻裘。

（六）七煞

资生利转多，贪婪意不休。为锱铢舍命寻争斗。
田连阡陌心犹窄，架插诗书眼不瞅。
也学采东篱菊，子是个装呵元亮，豹子浮丘。

（七）六煞

恨不得扬子江变做酒，枣穰金积到斗。
为几文赇背钱，受了些旁人咒。
一斗粟与亲眷分了颜面，
二斤麻把相知结下寇仇。
真伱缪，一味的骄而且吝，甚的是乐以忘忧！

(八）五煞

这财曾燃了董卓脐，曾枭了元载头。
聚而不散遭殃咎。
怕不是堆金积玉连城富，
眨眼早野草闲花满地愁。
干生受，生财有道，受用无由。

（九）四煞

有一日大小运并在命宫，死囚限缠在卯酉。
甚的散得疾，子为你聚来得骤。
恰待调和新曲歌金帐，逼临得佳人坠玉楼。
难收救，一壁厢投河奔井，一壁厢烂额焦头。

（十）三煞

窗隔每都飑飑的飞，椅桌每都出出的走。
金银钱米都消为尘垢。
山魈木客相呼唤，寡宿孤辰厮趁逐。
喧白昼，花月妖将家人狐媚，虚耗鬼把仓库潜偷。

（十一）二煞

恼天公降下灾，犯官刑系在囚。
他用钱时难参透。待买他上木驴
钉子轻轻钉，吊脊筋钩儿浅浅钩。
便用杀难宽宥，魂飞荡荡，魄散悠悠。

(十二)尾

出落他平生聚敛的情,都写做临刑犯罪由。
将他死骨头告示向通衢里甃,
任他日炙风吹慢慢朽。

孙周卿

蟾宫曲

山居自乐

草团标正对山凹,山竹炊粳,山水煎茶。
山芋山薯,山葱山韭,山果山花。
山溜响冰敲月牙,扫山云惊散林鸦。
山色元佳,山景堪夸。山外晴霞,山下人家。

曹德

庆东原

江头即事

低茅舍,卖酒家,客来旋把朱帘挂。
长天落霞,方池睡鸭,老树昏鸦。
几句杜陵诗,一幅王维画。

真氏

解三酲

奴本是明珠擎掌,怎生的流落平康?
对人前乔做作娇模样,背地里泪千行。
三春南国怜飘荡,一事东风无主张。
添悲怆,那里有珍珠十斛,来赎云娘?

吴西逸

天净沙

闲题

长江万里归帆,西风几度阳关?依旧红尘满眼。
夕阳新雁,此情时拍阑干。

清江引

秋居

白云乱飞秋似雪,清露生凉夜。
扫却石边云,醉踏松根月,星斗满天人睡也。

寿阳曲

四时(秋)

索心事,惹恨词。更那堪动人秋思?
画楼边几声新雁儿,不传书摆成个愁字。

程景初

醉太平

恨绵绵深宫怨女,情默默梦断羊车,
冷清清长门寂寞长青芜。
日迟迟春风院宇,泪漫漫介破琅玕玉。
闷淹淹散心出户闲凝伫,
昏惨惨晚烟妆点雪模糊,
渐零零洒梨花暮雨。

无名氏

水仙子

(一)

青山隐隐水茫茫,时节登高却异乡。
孤城孤客孤舟上,铁石人也断肠。
泪涟涟断送了秋光。
黄花梦,一夜香,过了重阳。

(二)

夕阳西下水东流,一事无成两鬓秋。
伤心人比黄花瘦,怯重阳九月九。
强登临情思悠悠。
望故国三千里,倚秋风十二楼,没来由惹起闲愁。

（三）
常记的离筵饮泣饯行时，折尽青青杨柳枝。
欲拈斑管书心事，无那可乾坤天样般纸。
意悬悬诉不尽相思，漫写下鸳鸯字，
空吟就花月词，凭何人付与娇姿？

折桂令

（一）

叹世间多少痴人，多是忙人，少是闲人。
酒色迷人，财气昏人，缠定活人。
钹儿鼓儿终日送人，车儿马儿常时迎人。
精细的瞒人，本分的饶人。
不识时人，枉只为人。

（二）微雪

朔风寒吹下银沙，蠹砌穿帘，拂柳惊鸦。
轻若鹅毛，娇如柳絮，瘦似梨花。
多应是怜贫困天教少洒，
止不过庆丰年众与农家。
数片琼葩，点缀槎丫。
孟浩然容易寻梅，陶学士不够烹茶。

塞鸿秋

（一）山行警

东边路，西边路，南边路。
五里铺，七里铺，十里铺。
行一步，盼一步，懒一步。
霎时间天也暮，日也暮，云也暮。
斜阳满地铺，回首生烟雾。
兀的不山无数，水无数，情无数。

（二）

爱他时似爱初生月，喜他时似喜看梅梢月
想他时道几首西江月，盼他时似盼辰钩月。
当初意儿别，今日相抛撒，
要相逢似水底捞明月。

梧叶儿

（一）嘲谎人

东村里鸡生凤，南庄上马变牛。六月里裹皮裘。
瓦垄上宜栽树，阳沟里好驾舟。
瓮来大肉馒头，俺家的茄子大如斗。

（二）贪

一夜千条计，百年万世心。火院有海来深。
头枕着连城玉，脚踩着遍地金。
有一日死来临，问贪公那一件儿替得您？

四换头

（一）相思

两叶眉头，怎锁相思万种愁？
从他别后，无心挑绣，这般证候，天知道和天瘦。

（二）约情

东墙花月，好景良宵恁记着。
低低的说：来时节，明日早些，不志诚随灯灭！

红绣鞋

（一）

一个日请千钟美禄，一个家无儋石之储。
天理如何有荣枯？
一个三十二上居陋巷，一个二十四考做中书，
都做了北邙山下土。

（二）

裁剪下才郎名讳，端详了展转伤悲。
把两个字灯焰上燎成灰，
或擦在双鬓角，或画着远山眉，
则要我眼跟前常见你。

（三）

一两句别人闲话，三四日不把门踏。
五六日不来呵在谁家？七八遍买龟儿卦，
久以后见他么，十分的憔悴煞。

（四）赠妓

长江水流不尽心事，中条山隔不断情思。
想着你，夜深沉，人静悄，自来时。
来时节三两句话，去时节一篇词，
记在你心窝儿里直到死。

庆宣和

寄语寒窗老秀才,一经头白,
更等甚三年选场开?去来,去来!

沉醉东风

(一)
安排下歌喉舞腰,准备着月夕花朝。
恨春过,伤春早,
且休教燕莺知道,春色三分二分了。
莫惜花前醉倒。

(二)
俺三竿日身披衲甲,恁五更寒帽裹乌纱。
俺耕耘阔角牛,恁嘶月高头马。
俺打勤劳不羡荣华,恁苦战垓心血染沙。
俺老瓦盆边醉煞。

塞儿令

有钱时唤小哥,无钱也失人情。
好家私伴着些歹后生,卖弄他聪明。
一关的胡行。踢气球养鹌鹑,解库中不想营生。
包服内响钞精钞,但行处,十数个花街里做郎君
则由他胡子传柳隆卿。

上小楼

杜鹃

堪恨无情杜宇,你怎么伤人心绪?
啼的花残,叫的愁来,唤将春去。
索甚不把离人叮咛嘱咐,我也道在天涯不如归去。

寄生草

有几句知心话,本待要诉与他。
对神前剪下青丝发,背爷娘暗约在湖山下。
冷清清,湿透凌波袜,恰相逢和我意儿差。
不剌你不来时,还我香罗帕。

快活三过朝天子四换头

（一）快活三

良辰媚景换今古，赏心乐事暗乘除。
人生四事岂能无？不可教轻辜负。

（二）朝天子
唤取伴侣，正好向西湖路。
花前沉醉倒玉壶，香瀲雾，红飞雨。
九十韶华，人间客寓。
把三分分数数：
一分是流水，二分是尘土，不觉的春将暮。

（三）四换头

西园杖屦，望眼无穷恨有余。
飘残香絮，歌残白纻。
海棠花底鹧鸪，杨柳梢头杜宇，
都唤取春归去。

阅金经

一竿为活计，往来西又东。
笑着荷衣不叹穷。
翁，醉眠杨柳风。
波微动，晚来舟自横。

普天乐

他生的脸儿峥,庞儿正。
诸余里耍俏,所事里聪明。
忒可憎,没薄幸。
行里坐里茶里饭里和随定,
恰便似纸幡儿引了人魂灵。
想那些个滋滋味味,风风韵韵,老老成成。

雁儿落过得胜令

(一)雁儿落

一年老一年,一日没一日。
一秋又一秋,一辈催一辈。

(二)得胜令

一聚一离别,一喜一伤悲。
一榻一身卧,一生一梦里。
寻一伙相识,他一会,咱一会;
都一般相知,吹一回,唱一回。

叨叨令

（一）
黄尘万古长安路，折碑三尺邙山墓。
西风一叶乌江渡，夕阳十里邯郸树。
老了人也么哥，老了人也么哥，
英雄尽是伤心处。

（二）
溪边小径舟横渡，门前流水清如玉。
青山隔断红尘路，白云满地无寻处。
说与你寻不得也么哥，寻不得也么哥，
却原来侬家鹦鹉洲边住。

（三）
不思量尤在心头记，越思量越恁地添憔悴。
香罗帕揾不住腮边泪。
几时节笑吟吟，成了鸳鸯配？
兀的不盼杀人也么哥！兀的不盼杀人也么哥！
咱两个武陵溪畔，曾相识。

游四门

（一）
落红满地湿胭脂，游赏正宜时。
呆才料不顾蔷薇刺。贪折海棠枝。
支！抓破绣裙儿。

（二）
海棠花下月明时，有约暗通私。
不付能等得红娘至。欲审旧题诗。
支！关上角门儿。

三番玉楼人

风摆檐间马，雨打响碧窗纱，枕剩衾寒没乱煞。
不着我题名儿骂。
暗想他，忒情杂，等来家，好生的歹斗咱。
我将那厮脸儿上不抓，
耳轮儿揪罢，我问你昨夜宿谁家？

朝天子
志感

不读书有权,不识字有钱,不晓事倒有人夸荐。
老天只恁忒心偏,贤和愚无分辨。
折挫英雄,消磨良善,越聪明越运蹇。
志高如鲁连,德过如闵骞,
依本分只落的人轻贱。

红绣鞋

窗外雨声声不住,枕边泪点点长吁。
雨声泪点急相逐,雨声儿添凄惨,泪点儿助长吁。
枕边泪倒多如窗外雨。

喜春来
闺情

窄裁衫褪安排瘦,淡扫蛾眉准备愁。
思君一度一登楼。凝望久,雁过楚天秋。

快活三过朝天子四换头
忆别

（一）快活三

人去后敛翠颦,春归也掩朱门。
日长庭静怕黄昏,又是愁时分。

（二）朝天子

新痕,旧痕,泪滴尽愁难尽。
今宵鸳帐睡怎稳?口儿念心儿印,
独上妆楼,无人存问。
见花梢月半轮,望频,断魂。
正人远天涯近。

（三）四换头

长空成阵,雁字行行点暮云。
早是多离多恨,多愁多闷。
叮咛的嘱君:
若见俺那人,早寄取个平安信。

骂玉郎过感皇恩采茶歌

（一）骂玉郎

四时唯有春无价，尊日月富年华。
垂杨影里人如画。
锦一攒，绣一堆，在秋千下。

（二）感皇恩

语笑忻恰，炒闹喧哗。
软红乡，簇定个，小宫娃。
彩绳款拈，画板轻踏，
微着力，身慢举，拽裙纱。

（三）采茶歌

众矜夸，是交加。彩云飞上日边霞。
体态轻盈那闲雅，精神羞落树头花。

Theory on Literary Translation of the Chinese School

The theory on literary translation of the Chinese school owes its origin to traditional Chinese culture, including the Confucian and the Taoist school of thought respectively represented by *Thus Spoke the Master* and *Laws Divine and Human*.

It is said in the first chapter of *Laws Divine and Human* that truth can be known, but it may not be the truth you know, and that things may be named, but names are not the things. When applied to literary translation, this may mean that the theory on literary translation can be known, but it may not the unproven theory on the one hand, nor the scientific theory on the other, for neither literary translation nor its theory is science. As the names are not equal to the things, the translation cannot be equal to the original. As there is more difference than equivalence between the Chinese and the English language, the principle of equivalence can not be applied to the translation between them as between two occidental languages.

It is said in the last chapter of *Laws Divine and Human* that truthful words may not be beautiful and beautiful words may not be truthful. That is to say, there is contradiction between truth and beauty or between equivalence and excellence. A translation where equivalents are used may be called a faithful or truthful translation. When no equivalent can be found between two languages, the translator should make use of the best expressions or excellent expressions of the target language. That may be called theory of excellence.

In *Thus Spoke the Master*, Confucius said, "At seventy, I can do what I will without going beyond what is right." Professor Zhu Guangqian said that this has shown the mature state of an artist. I think it may also show the mature state of a literary translator. The literal translator has used the equivalents without going beyond the original in sound; the liberal translator has described the image without going beyond the original in sense; the literary translator has described the scene without going beyond reality. Not to go beyond the original is to be truthful or faithful, and the translator has reached the ordinary level of translation. To do what one will without going beyond the original is not only to be faithful but also to make his translation beautiful, in that case the translator has attained a higher level. To excel the original without going beyond the reality it describes is to attain the highest level.

What is literary translation? It is an art of solving the contradiction between faithfulness (or truth) and beauty. How to solve it? There are three methods, namely, equalization, generalization and particularization. When there is little or no contradition between truth and beauty, equalization or equivalents may be used. When there is contradction between them, generalization may be used to make the meaning clear, and particularization to make a deeper impression.

Confucius said in *Thus Spoke the Master* that it would be good to be understandable, better to be enjoyable and best to be delectable or delightful. When applied to literary translation, this principle means that an understandable translation is good, an enjoyable one is better and a delightful one is best. The ontology or theory of contradiction between truth and beauty, the methodology or theory of equalization, generalization and particularization, and the teleology or theory of the understandable, the enjoyable and the delectable, all owe their origin to the Confucian and Taoist schools of thoughts.

But Confucius said less about what delight is and more about how to be delightful. In the beginning of *Thus Spoke the Master* he said it is delightful to acquire knowledge and put it into practice; In Chapter Six he told us how Yan Hui could find delight in reading though living in a humble lane with only a handful of rice to eat and a gourdful of water to drink; In Chapter Eleven, Zeng Xi told us his delight in an spring excursion. From these examples we can see Confucius' theory on delight or teleology, and his theory on practice or methodology. His theory is not scientific but artistic. Since literary translation is an art but not a branch of science, his theory can not only be applied to the practice but also to the theory of literary translation. As his theory has stood the test of time, it is as durable as scientific theories. A theorist on science who studies truth and the truthful should not go beyond what is truthful. A theorist on art or an artist who studies beauty and the beautiful may go beyond what is truthful and faithful.

The contradiction between truth and beauty in Chinese theory on literary translation has developed into a contradiction between equivalence and excellence. As Keats said, "Beauty is truth, truth beauty," we may even say beauty is a virtue, a kind of excellence. When we cannot find the equivalent, we may resort to generalization or particularization.

In short, literary translation is an art to create the beautiful. This is the epistemology of the Chinese school. The contradiction between truth and beauty or between equivalence and excellence is its ontology; the theory on equalization, generalization and particularization is its triple methodology; and the theory of the understandable, the enjoyable and the delectable or delightful is its triple teleology.

Xu Yuanchong
Oct. 2011

代后记：中国学派的文学翻译理论

中国学派的文学翻译理论源自中国的传统文化，主要包括儒家思想和道家思想，儒家思想的代表著作是《论语》，道家思想的代表著作是《老子道德经》。

《老子道德经》第一章开始就说："道可道，非常道；名可名，非常名。"联系到翻译理论上来，就是说：翻译理论是可以知道的，是可以说得出来的，但不是只说得出来而经不起实践检验的空头理论，这就是中国学派翻译理论中的实践论。其次，文学翻译理论不能算科学理论（自然科学），与其说是社会科学理论，不如说是人文学科或艺术理论，这就是文学翻译的艺术论，也可以说是相对论。后六个字"名可名，非常名"应用到文学翻译理论上来，可以有两层意思：第一层是原文的文字是描写现实的，但并不等于现实，文字和现实之间还有距离，还有矛盾；第二层意思是译文和原文之间也有距离，也有矛盾，译文和原文所描写的现实之间，自然还有距离，还有矛盾。译文应该发挥译语优势，运用最好的译语表达方式，来和原文展开竞赛，使译文和现实的距离或矛盾小于原文和现实之间的矛盾，那就是超越原文了。这就是文学翻译理论中的优势论或优化论，超越论或竞赛论。文学翻译理论应该解决的不只是译文和原文在文字方面的矛盾，还要解决译文和原文所反映的现实之间的矛盾，这是文学翻译的本体论。

一般翻译只要解决"真"或"信"或"似"的问题，文学翻译却要解决"真"或"信"和"美"之间的矛盾。原文反映的现实不只是言内之意,还有言外之意。中国的文学语言往往有言外之意,甚至还有言外之情。文学翻译理论也要解决译文和原文的言外之意、言外之情的矛盾。

《论语》说:"知之者不如好之者,好之者不如乐之者。"知之,好之,乐之,这"三之论"是对艺术论的进一步说明。艺术论第一条原则要求译文忠实于原文所反映的现实,求的是真,可以使人知之;第二条原则要求用"三化"法来优化译文,求的是美,可以使人好之;第三条原则要求用"三美"来优化译文,尤其是译诗词,求的是意美、音美和形美,可以使人乐之。如果"不逾矩"的等化译文能使人知之(理解),那就达到了文学翻译的低标准,如从心所欲而不逾矩的浅化或深化的译文既能使人知之,又能使人好之(喜欢),那就达到了中标准;如果从心所欲的译文不但能使人知之,好之,还能使人乐之(愉快),那才达到了文学翻译的高标准。这也是中国译者对世界译论作出的贡献。

翻译艺术的规律是从心所欲而不逾矩。"矩"就是规矩,规律。但艺术规律却可以依人的主观意志而转移,是因为得到承认才算正确的。所以贝多芬说:为了更美,没有什么清规戒律不可打破。他所说的戒律不是科学规律,而是艺术规律。不能用科学规律来评论文学翻译。

孔子不大谈"什么是"(What?)而多谈"怎么做"(How?)。这是中国传统的方法论,比西方流传更久,影响更广,作用更大,并且经过了两三千年实践的考验。《论语》第一章中说:"学而时习之,不亦说(悦,乐)乎!""学"是取得知识,"习"是实践。孔子只说学习实践可以得到乐趣,却不说什么是"乐"。这就是孔子的方法论,是中国文学翻译理论的依据。

总而言之,中国学派的文学翻译理论是研究老子提出的

"信"（似）"美"（优）矛盾的艺术（本体论），但"信"不限原文，还指原文所反映的现实，这是认识论，"信"由严复提出的"信达雅"发展到鲁迅提出"信顺"的直译，再发展到陈源的"三似"（形似，意似，神似），直到傅雷的"重神似不重形似"，这已经接近"美"了。"美"发展到鲁迅的"三美"（意美，音美，形美），再发展到林语堂提出的"忠实，通顺，美"，转化为朱生豪"传达原作意趣"的意译，直到茅盾提出的"美的享受"。孔子提出的"从心所欲"发展到郭沫若提出的创译论（好的翻译等于创作），以及钱钟书说的译文可以胜过原作的"化境"说，再发展到优化论，超越论，"三化"（等化，浅化，深化）方法论。孔子提出的"不逾矩"和老子说的"信言不美，美言不信"有同有异。老子"信美"并重，孔子"从心所欲"重于"不逾矩"，发展为朱光潜的"艺术论"，包括郭沫若说的"在信达之外，愈雅愈好。所谓'雅'不是高深或讲修饰，而是文学价值或艺术价值比较高。"直到茅盾说的："必须把文学翻译工作提高到艺术创造的水平。"孔子的"乐之"发展为胡适之的"愉快"说（翻译要使读者读得愉快），再发展到"三之"（知之，好之，乐之）目的论。这就是中国学派的文学翻译理论发展为"美化之艺术"（"三美"，"三化"，"三之"的艺术）的概况。

许渊冲
2011年10月

图书在版编目（CIP）数据

元曲三百首: 汉英对照 / 许渊冲译. —2版. —北京: 五洲传播出版社, 2019.6
ISBN 978-7-5085-4206-5

Ⅰ.①元… Ⅱ.①许… Ⅲ.①元曲－选集－汉、英 Ⅳ.①I222.9

中国版本图书馆CIP数据核字(2019)第098670号

元曲三百首

译　者：	许渊冲
策划编辑：	荆孝敏　郑　磊
责任编辑：	王　峰
中文编辑：	张　梅
英文编辑：	北　塔
装帧设计：	北京正视文化艺术有限责任公司
出版发行：	五洲传播出版社
地　　址：	北京市海淀区北三环中路31号生产力大楼B座6层
邮　　编：	100088
电　　话：	010-82005927，010-82007837
网　　址：	http://www.cicc.org.cn　http://www.thatsbooks.com
印　　刷：	中煤（北京）印务有限公司
版　　次：	2012年1月第1版　2019年6月第2版第1次印刷
开　　本：	140mm×210mm　1/32
印　　张：	10.25
字　　数：	280千字
书　　号：	ISBN 978-7-5085-4206-5
定　　价：	89.00元